WHERE THE BOYS ARE

EDITED BY
RICHARD LABONTÉ

Cleis Press Inc., P.O. Box 14697, San Francisco, California 94114.

Printed in the United States.
Cover design: Scott Idleman
Cover photograph: Stockbyte/Getty
Text design: Frank Wiedemann
Cleis logo art: Juana Alicia
First Edition.
10 9 8 7 6 5 4 3 2 1

For Asa, from California to Canada,
my migrating man

Contents

INTRODUCTION

Some of the stories in *Where the Boys Are* are about physical migration, from small town to big city, from straight neighborhood to gay neighborhood; others are about a more emotional migration, the transition from questioning to queer, from out there alone to, finally, "out" among others.

And the thread that runs through all of them, of course, is the exploration of that queer moment where you ask yourself where you fit in. And then you go find where that is.

That moment can come at any age, a reality reflected in this collection. In a majority of these stories, it comes when younger men grapple with an unsettled identity and an inchoate yearning. Those are the kind of fellows, some still teens, others in their twenties, in Rachel Kramer Bussel's "Live from New York," Kemble Scott's "Unable to Hold Back," Sam J. Miller's "My Evil Twin," Jameson Currier's "One of the Guys," Zeke Mangold's "God Hates Techno," Ted Cornwell's "Local Fame," and Alana Noel Voth's "Juniper House"—seven tales about that first tingle of sexual initiation. About finding where the boys are, and finally fitting in.

Some of the characters start out in their own queer skins: the Southern lad new to New York in Douglas A. Martin's "Other Residences, Other Neighborhoods," who makes the city his sexual playground; another Southern lad new to New York in Lee Houck's "Tiny Golden Kernel," for whom sex is easy, love less so; and the edgy Sex Pistols–era London punk in Erastes' "Drug Colors," who can have any eager fag-puppy he wants, but yearns for a man less attainable. They've found where the boys are; the next step is sorting out the sex, perhaps finding love.

And for some, the boys aren't found until later in life: that's the way it is in Dale Chase's "Half-Life," about a married man who confronts his needs after surviving a heart attack. For others, it was wide open early—as in Simon Sheppard's reflective "Wild Night."

The working title for this anthology was *City Boys*, and it was first conceived as a sort-of sequel to the earlier Cleis collection *Country Boys*, stories about coming out and being queer away from big cities and their gay enclaves. Despite its different title, it remains an anthology about physical, emotional, and sexual exploration by gay men—about their migration toward urban centers, into their queer identity. Two of the stories here, however, Jeff Mann's "Taming the Trees" and Alpha Martial's "The Birds and the Bees," offer a been-there, done-that twist on the topic: they're both about gay men in vigorous midlife who learned a lot from their time in the city—but who have decided in the end that they "fit in" better away from the gayborhood. And why not? It's all part of the life that follows discovering *Where the Boys Are*. Here are stories of first-time sex and the loves of a lifetime, of being seduced by the city and its sexual possibilities, of learning how to read the codes that define contemporary queer life.

Many thanks to Jules Chamberlain, a fine friend in the middle of his own migration.

Richard Labonté

LIVE FROM NEW YORK

Rachel Kramer Bussel

I didn't expect to get my cock sucked on my first night in New York City, but maybe I should have. It wasn't that I hadn't dreamed about the glittery, magical, overpowering gay mecca that everyone in the world seemed to want to get to and make their own. Visions of Christopher Street danced in my head from the time I became too old for sugarplums. I knew there were hot, hunky guys, as well as huge, hairy ones, but that's pretty much where my imagery stopped; chiseled and flawless or fat and furry, those were the choices. I didn't know which one was my type, but it didn't really matter. I truly did not think any of them would want anything to do with me.

Let me back up a minute. Some people decide to up and move when the weather's sunny and warm, taking their time driving cross-country, relishing the lazy outdoors. Me, I like to move in the dead of winter. Something about the chilly air stirs up my wanderlust. I've lived in plenty of cities in my thirty-plus years, but none can beat the one I return to again and again: New

York. I have an apartment here that's only gone up in worth, but to me, it's priceless. Whenever I return, I feel the city's fabric closing tight around me, zipping me in, layering me with the protection only a mixed-up, mashed-up, melting pot of craziness can provide. The night I moved here still rings in my ears, sometimes literally. I'll hear the cheers of a crowd at a ball game roaring like they get a prize for making the most noise, and remember landing in the Big Apple on New Year's Eve 1993, with just a backpack on my back and a cock ready, willing and eager; hopeful, even.

I came here from a hick town most people have never heard of, and even if you had, you'd want to forget about it just as quickly as you could. Sure, the people were generous and good-hearted, as long as you wore the right kinds of clothes, said the right kinds of things, and didn't act remotely in any way like you might maybe, possibly be gay. Or bi. Or even have considered such possibilities. If you had, and were anything above completely idiotic, you kept your mouth shut.

So I did, often pressing my lips tightly together as I jerked off to forbidden images that nevertheless came unbidden into my head. This was just before the days when hot man-on-man action was available at the click of a mouse, so I had to make do with the meager offerings of the men around me, and by offerings, I mean fantasy fodder, not any actual experimentation. I learned fast how to play "spot the gay," but back then, I was sure I was the only one.

I was a virgin, in every sense of the word, when my bus pulled into town. I'd never even gone all the way with a girl. Yes, I took the bus from Buttfuck, Middle America to Port Authority, on one of the coldest New Year's Eves in recent history. I was able to get away by saying I was going to the big bonfire, which was really a place where drunk kids stripped naked, drank vodka, ran into the lake and fucked their brains out. I'd been to enough of those and had to fend off girls wanting me to touch them everywhere to know I couldn't stand one more night of it.

But when I got off the bus in the city, I could hear the crowd buzzing. It was ten and the streets all around Times Square, and seemingly in the whole city, were paved with people. People of all kinds, speaking all different languages; families, pretty girls, old men, drag queens, anyone and everyone.

I tried not to stare in too much awe, and started walking. I found myself entering a Ben & Jerry's, suddenly eager for something sweet. I walked in and immediately felt self-conscious. This was nothing like my hometown ice-cream shop, and as much as I'd privately derided my neighbors as the biggest hicks around, suddenly *I* was the biggest hick, at least the biggest one about to buy a vanilla cone. I chose a waffle cone just to somehow differentiate my order, and at the last second, went for chocolate chip. All of a sudden, I felt silly, like I should be eating something more manly, more macho, to celebrate my newfound independence. I was gay but did that mean I had to be a sissy? No sooner had I handed over my four dollars than I felt someone brush against me.

"That's a big cone," a male voice said. For a second, I felt like a child being berated for taking seconds when we had six mouths to feed. But one look at the man stopped me in my tracks. He was older than me, at least twice my age. His skin was tan, and tough, somehow, but his blue eyes were kind. He had dirty-blond stubble, but not a beard, and looked like maybe he worked outdoors. His clothes were nothing special, jeans and a black T-shirt, with sneakers, but he was staring at me so intently I thought I must have done something wrong.

"Long bus ride, I needed some energy," I said, wanting to smile but not sure if that was proper. I didn't even know what this man wanted, but already I'd gotten hard. I really wasn't looking for sex, at least not directly. I was looking for it by coming to New York, but I figured it could wait a day. For one night, I wanted to be a good old-fashioned American tourist, albeit a gay one, but nobody could tell about that, right? Wrong. This man could tell. And he apparently planned to watch me eat every bite of my cone. He moved aside to let me get some napkins, but when I sat down, he sat too, facing me.

"I'm Jared," he said. "I came here on a bus once, too." I didn't know then that we were right near Hell's Kitchen, which wasn't quite Chelsea or Christopher Street but still had its fair share of homos. I didn't know then that I'd wind up living mere blocks away with my first boyfriend a year later. I didn't know that I looked as gay as you could get, everything from my haircut to my Converse sneakers to the hunger on my face, signals I'd later come to read on college boys and those way too young for me who were nevertheless irresistible. They say we can never truly judge ourselves.

I let Jared watch me eat my cone while people hustled in and out, eager for a last-minute snack before watching the ball drop. He made conversation, told me his life story, something about being a marathon runner; by now, it's all kind of faded, considering that I never saw him again. You'd think I'd have been listening, rapt with attention, to a real live gay guy. I probably would have, if I'd known that's who I was talking to. For all the gaydar I assumed I possessed simply as a birthright, I had no clue. I just thought he was friendly, a little lonely, a good sport, so I sat there and ate the huge waffle cone until I could practically breathe vanilla through my nostrils. I threw out the last little bit of the cone and willed my stomach not to heave.

That cone was probably what kept me from getting drunk off my ass that night; somehow, the flask that Jared had tucked away in his coat pocket didn't seem appealing. When I declined, he took a small sip, then put it back. "Southern Comfort," he said, laughing as if to himself. Maybe he thought I was from the South, or that was just what he was drinking, I don't really know.

He kept on talking, his steady stream of conversation making me feel gradually more at home, like it was just another noise designed to comfort me. Oh, how true that was, because while I was barely listening, I was still somehow hard as a rock. Maybe it came from just knowing that it was okay to have a dick and have a vague clue what to do with it in this freak-show, anything-goes city where men were beating their chests and chugging beer like the world was going to end and women were stripping like we were at Mardi Gras, except without the beads. Maybe just having a man paying attention to me like that, watching me, waiting, gave me permission to own my hard-on. Or maybe I just needed to have my dick sucked. Who really knows? What I do know is that as it got closer to midnight, Jared got increasingly quiet. We never kissed or anything like that. He just kept looking at me, as if waiting for my okay.

By the time I finally realized what was going down, as it were, I almost came in my pants. I mean, who really expects shit like this to happen to them? Not me, back then, that was for sure. Jared didn't look like what I thought the gay guys were supposed to. He didn't have the uniform, the talk, the walk, the cues I'd picked up watching prime-time TV. He didn't grab me and throw me up against the bathroom wall of the Ben & Jerry's, even though later I'd come to find that I liked it quite a bit when men grabbed me and threw me against walls, beds, floors, anything that was hard and firm and would make me meet it with every nerve ending I possessed. My night with Jared, if you can call it a night, though it was really more accurately an encounter, had nothing kinky about it. It was almost gentle, as if the city in all its big gay glory was saying, "Welcome. You're home. Now go get laid." Because the quieter Jared got, the closer he came to me, until he was stroking the shorn sides of my head, running his hand over my chest, then lower.

The crowd was too preoccupied to care what two quiet men off to the side of a barricade were doing, and anyone who noticed either pretended not to or, for all I knew, got quite the peep show. As the hubbub reached fever pitch, with the last minutes of the year practically vanishing before our eyes, Jared sank to his knees and, without a word, unzipped my jeans and took my cock in his mouth. He did it so smoothly and silently—like it was all one motion, zipperhandcockmouth—that I almost forgot I'd never had it done to me before. I'd dreamt and fantasized and wondered and questioned, but nothing could have prepared me for Jared's expert lips wrapped around my hardness. His hot wet mouth sucking, seeking, soothing. His tongue tracing my length, speaking all the words he couldn't say. I didn't need "I want you," or "I like you," or "You're hot," at least not then. Now, yes, I can't concede without a little flirtation. But that night, Jared was perfect, not just the way he moved his lips, but the way his body met mine, assuring me everything would be okay. The ball dropped, my balls tightened and rose, and soon I was spurting right into Jared's mouth.

I gasped and then all too quickly it was over. I was tucked back in, Jared had wiped his mouth and was staring off into the distance. At what or whom I didn't ask, and he didn't tell. It was the highest high and then not so much a low as a plateau, a glimpse into the future of lonely nights following outrageously hot sex. As short as it was, Jared had given me one of the best blow jobs of my life, and not just because I had nothing to compare it to.

The crowd roared with a New Year's high of its own; Jared looked at me a bit wistfully, like he wanted to stay and chat but had somewhere else to be. Maybe he did. He gave me the name of a hotel nearby, and when I could make it past the revelers, I walked to my temporary new home, getting a tired smile from the clerk. I was sure he could tell not just that I was gay, but that I'd just gotten a blow job in Times Square. I was sure everyone could tell and for the first time in my life, I liked that feeling. No more secrets, no more shame, his look seemed to say. We don't do that here. Welcome to New York. And Happy New Year.

UNABLE TO HOLD BACK

Kemble Scott

Vacne. That was the word Raphe struggled to remember. Those tiny red blotches of nascent pimples surrounding a guy's mouth. When a friend told Raphe the nickname for it he laughed out loud. *Vagina* plus *acne* equals *vacne*, the minor outbreak caused by a man going down on a woman.

The man next to him on the BART platform definitely had vacne. He was average height, with black razor stubble. His hair was dark, with just enough gel to keep it professionally in place and defy the notorious winds of downtown.

The man's pin stripe suit made Raphe's mind flash to what happened at the urinals in the bathroom at McDonalds. He always got a sick feeling whenever he remembered that moment. The embarrassment. How awful to be caught looking.

The incident had cured him of wandering eyes. To be sure of that, Raphe brought his laptop to work at the mailbox shop to keep him busy during the slow times, and to finally start writing his long-delayed novel.

That was two weeks ago, and Raphe still hadn't typed a word of his book. He'd get too distracted. First he'd check his e-mail. Then he had to get caught up on the latest news from sfgate.com. Next was a link from a friend to a hysterical story about online dating. "The odds are good, but the goods are odd." A spam brought him to a site called rotton.com, which led him to learning about a Japanese fetish called bukkake. Sick!

One day he went to craigslist.org to put up for sale the IKEA carpet he never really liked. He could use the money. While there he began to peruse the other classified ads, eyeing cars he would buy if he ever had money again. He checked the Help Wanted section, but didn't find anything even remotely worthwhile. Just a Pink Slip Party. He wasn't that desperate—at least not yet.

Then he hit the personal ads. He'd never explored them before. Why bother? There were a billion guys just like him in The City these days. Having a SoMa condo, tech stock options, and a degree from Brown once got a guy laid at places like the infamous meat market bar Elroy's. That place was long gone, the stock options now worthless, and the degree meaningless until attached to a paycheck. At twenty-five, was he supposed to feel so washed up?

He turned to the Casual Encounters section of the web site: no strings attached sexual experiences for men and women. Maybe that would make him feel better. He hadn't had sex since Lisa, and that was nearly a year ago. He'd been on only one date since then, and she only wanted to cuddle. For hours Raphe read the listings, amazed at what people had the nerve to advertise. Three ways. Erotic massages. *K-9*?

A few times he answered the tamer ads, using a Hotmail account he created to obscure his identity. To his surprise, many people answered back. But when they asked for a photograph he chickened out. Are there really women who like to do these things? Or are they just collecting photographs of idiots stupid enough to respond to their postings? He imagined girls huddled around a cubicle in an office somewhere giggling over which dorks had dared to send in the most revealing shots of themselves.

Then he found a listing with remarkably simple copy. The message contained just one word. “BART.” He knew that stood for Bay Area Rapid Transit, the commuter train service that connected The City to the suburbs. What “casual encounter” could possibly happen in such a public place?

The word “BART” was tinted blue, making it a hyperlink. With a click, Raphe found himself transported into a Yahoo group called BARTM4M. M4M—men for men. A gay site. He quickly closed down the browser, ashamed that somewhere in his computer’s memory would be a record that he visited such a web site.

As he closed the laptop, a sensation hit—that he was being watched. He looked up toward the front window, catching sight of the woman with red hair from upstairs. Raphe threw an animated smile in her direction, but she had already turned and the moment was lost. Had she been looking at him? If so, for how long? Is it possible she saw him looking at *that web site*? No, he chided himself. She wouldn’t be able to see the screen from there. He was just being paranoid. Raphe continued to stare at the red-haired woman as she faded into the distance. How beautiful she was, even while walking away. She was wearing that pastel green pullover again, the one that showed off her athletic build. He loved that top. He knew it would be in her clothing rotation at least once a month.

Dammit. He wasn’t *gay*. What was so bad about looking at that web site? It made no sense for someone completely straight to feel threatened by such things. Besides, maybe he’d find material for his book. There was certainly nothing wrong with being curious. He'd never be a real writer if he didn't start to stretch his mind. BART was as good a place to start as any.

Raphe smiled to himself. She was checking him out—the red-haired woman from upstairs! He'd caught her. At least he thought he had.

Back on the web site, Raphe learned BARTM4M was a gathering place for men who enjoyed a specific sexual fetish, one intrinsically linked to the daily commute. At first, he wondered if it was a joke. But Yahoo counted more than three thousand registered members, leading Raphe to think it had to be real or one of the most elaborately staged hoaxes of all time.

If it was true, then it would make for a great story—a real shocker. The only way to find out would be to take the journey himself.

Raphe got into the underground BART station at the Embarcadero stop, uneasily walking past the loud homeless contingent that sat on the park benches next to the entrance. He'd heard that people from the offices nearby cruelly referred to each of the decrepit men as a "Solitaire," since they never seemed to see each other, instead shouting non-stop at invisible demons who tormented them. Still, Raphe liked coming downtown to soak up the energy, and wondered why he didn't visit more often. After all, he lived only a few blocks away in SoMa. He could see the steel and glass monetary monuments from the windows of his high-rise condo, sometimes musing about the busy lives of the swarms inside those business hives. After his meltdown in dot-com, he figured he was never built for the life of a corporate drone, but envied the simplicity and camaraderie of it.

The BARTM4M web site said the trip from The City to the East Bay took seven minutes. Seven minutes under the floor of the bay. An amazing engineering feat, Raphe thought. Whoever figured this out were geniuses. Surely, they'd be stunned to learn their invention was now nicknamed "the tunnel of love."

The last BART train. Not the last of the day, but the final cabin at the tail end of any of the dozens of trains that made the trip. In another era it might have been called the caboose.

To get on the last car, Raphe waited at the far west end of the platform. As he stood, he sized up the man with the vacne. He was definitely in the right spot for the BARTM4M fetish, and he was clearly straight—and not just because of the telltale pimples. The way he walked. He was a handsome ruggedly built Latino, somewhere around thirty, and devoid of any fey mannerisms. There was no way he was gay.

A train bound for the town of Fremont pulled up. Raphe got in and walked all the way to the back. It was the three-thirty train. Rush hour had yet to start. There was hardly a soul in the compartment.

Raphe sat in the final row, facing forward. He kept his sunglasses on, even though he wouldn't be seeing any sunlight for at least seven minutes. He felt more comfortable as an observer if it was impossible for others to see his eyes.

There were four benches in the back, each made to seat two passengers. They faced forward, two benches per row with an aisle down the center. The brown industrial fabric of the seats looked worn, and the matching carpet was faded and ripped in places. Still, Raphe thought it remarkably clean, seeing no trash or sordid stains. He noted how all the advertising on the walls had to do with AIDS. "HIV changed my life," proclaimed Magic Johnson, "but it doesn't keep me from living." Another poster pushed the next AIDS bike ride to Los Angeles charity fundraiser. Raphe saw them as warning signs and felt a slight twinge in his stomach. Maybe the managers of BART knew what goes on back here.

No one else sat in the entire back half of the compartment. The Latino with the vacne must have gotten on a different train. The doors closed and with a few hesitant nudges the train pulled away into the tunnel. Shortly after it picked up speed, a man from the far front rows walked to the back. Without ever looking at Raphe, he sat on the bench across the aisle. He immediately lifted a folded copy of the front section of the *San Francisco Chronicle* to his face.

Raphe felt an unexpected burst of flush. Did the man notice? He didn't seem to. He just sat in his nicely pressed khaki pants with open-necked blue dress shirt and stared straight into the day's headlines. Works in an office, Raphe figured. A brokerage, perhaps. Guys in that field really had to keep up with the news. So why was this guy glued to the front page of the *morning* newspaper? The man held that one article too close to his face. He must be vision-impaired, or the slowest reader in the world. Why didn't he turn a page? Or flip it around?

Then Raphe noticed the man's other hand. In the moments since he'd sat down, the man had discreetly cupped himself. His legs were spread apart unnaturally wide. It was a position that could easily be interpreted as the body language of a slob. No, it could be more than that. Maybe this was the first signal for something to start.

Raphe repositioned himself, mimicking the same slouch. He scratched below his fly.

The man did the same.

Fascinated, Raphe pulled the front of his pants.

Instantly, the man repeated the motion. His eyes never seemed to leave the text of the newsprint, and yet somehow the man saw everything.

Suddenly it hit Raphe. The newspaper was just a clever prop to obscure the truth—a trick not revealed on the web site. The man had really been watching the entire time through the reflections of the windows. Once the train had entered the dark tunnel, the black of the outside turned the interior glass into a mirror, allowing for an unobstructed view into the row. One could see everything without directly looking.

Still, it was just spreading, scratching and pulling—not enough for Raphe to be convinced there was anything more going on than a couple of guys just coincidentally being guys. He needed a more concrete signal. Something to tell him it was safe to go further.

Without taking off his sunglasses or saying a word, Raphe offered the one gesture he figured would be interpreted as a sign that it was okay to proceed. He turned toward the man…and smiled.

The man smiled back, again without ever losing sight of the paper. With his free hand, he unzipped his fly. In a matter of seconds, he reached inside and tugged until he revealed himself.

The sight rattled Raphe more than he anticipated, a rush surged up his entire body. Would the man reach across the aisle and touch him?

No. Raphe knew that much from the web site. This was all about "showing off." Many of the men who told their tales on the site actually claimed to be straight. They just enjoyed "getting off with buddies." The web site said full circle jerks sometimes broke out, with as many as ten guys pretending to be strap hangers but really forming a wall to prevent anyone forward from knowing what was happening in the back. There was even a listing that said a woman often frequented those final rows, hiking her skirt to expose and please herself. She was a regular, accepted by the pack, even if some of the guys would rather have each other.

Except for the possibility of being arrested by the BART police, it was the ultimate in safe sex.

Raphe hesitantly undid his own pants and fumbled to bring himself to the surface. It was much harder to do sitting than he'd figured, and he needed both hands. The man with the paper was so skilled he never lost the pretense that he was just a guy in the back reading a newspaper.

Finally the newspaper came down, and the man looked over to Raphe. Blue eyes and boyishly handsome with mousy blond curls, slightly receding. Just as Raphe made eye contact, the man squinted, his face contorted as if someone had sneaked up behind and pinched him. But no one was there. Instead, there was a white splash onto the opened front page of the waiting newspaper. The splattered headline: BUSH A CROWD PLEASER.

In moments, the man composed himself and packaged everything back into his khakis. As if nothing had occurred, he got up and returned to the front of the compartment. Raphe frantically put himself in order, which was nearly impossible since he was still fully aroused. He wiped a few beads of sweat from his forehead with his sleeve. Seconds later the train emerged from the dark into dreary Port Oakland, past acres of empty cargo containers, stranded from the economic collapse. Going nowhere, Raphe thought. *Just like me.*

He couldn't get off at the first stop, his excitement refusing to subside in time to stand up. He waited until the train reached Lake Merritt, where he crossed the platform to the far end to again seek the final rows of the next inbound line. As he walked, he looked down at the ground, trying to avoid being seen. A familiar feeling of guilt hit, something that always happened whenever he experienced any type of sex—a shame that went back to the time when he was thirteen and reading a copy of *Penthouse* with his best friend Scott. The explicit photos and graphic stories had aroused both boys into pleasing themselves. Scott's father walked into the room, catching them with their pants down. He ordered them to get dressed and sent Raphe home.

For days Raphe feared his parents' phone would ring and he would be destroyed. Both his mother and father were strict and managed their emotions tightly around Raphe. Their lives revolved around the many committees they served on at the local Methodist church, setting a standard of behavior for the family that bordered on pious. No son of theirs could be caught with pornography. Worse, Scott's family attended the same church, making his sin possible fodder for the entire congregation. Not just for reading pornography, but he was sure there would be an accusation that he and Scott were caught having sex, though they'd never even touched each other.

The devastating phone call from Scott's father never came. Instead, there was something much worse. Silence. A sword of impending doom dangled over Raphe's head for the rest of his years in his hometown, worried each time he saw Scott's father that his vice would be exposed to all. Sometimes he craved to have it brought out in the open and accept his punishment, just to rid himself of the anxiety of waiting. Raphe was too young to understand the New England tradition of burying feelings and secrets in order to avoid confrontation at all cost. An emotional scene would never erupt. Scott's father simply and sternly told his son that he was never to be alone again with Raphe. Ever.

As he got back on BART at the Lake Merritt station for the return trip to The City, Raphe's heart raced. Guilty feelings aside, he would take the trip again. On the next journey out to the suburbs the train was sure to be packed, with rush hour hitting full swing. He wondered how that would change what the BARTM4M followers did.

Raphe plunked down into the last section, this time on the

aisle, and shut his eyes. Just relax, he told himself. On the reverse commute, the train would be empty, so he'd spend the time making mental notes of what had already happened and commit them to memory—for the sake of his novel, of course.

It really would make a great story—a real shocker.

He heard steps coming toward him. Don't look. He felt the slight breeze of someone pass, and peeked in time to catch the glimpse of a man in dark clothes get into the window seat. The doors closed, and the train made its initial nudge. The man turned, looked over to Raphe and grinned. They knew each other. The familiar pin stripe suit. Those rugged Latino good looks. The same dark hair, with just a bit of gel, and that same mouth, surrounded by the same telltale trail of vacne.

"Are you following me?" Raphe stammered.

"Would you let me?" the man asked.

MY EVIL TWIN

Sam J. Miller

Solomon

Some churches have showers, but I don't like using them. They all have weird schedules—hard to keep track of and always changing. Even worse, they never have a safe place for you to put your stuff, you just throw it in a big pile in a corner of the room, and absolutely everyone has access to it. I'll be damned if I'm leaving my backpack and my only set of clothes in a big heap where every guy and girl can get to it.

Anyway I've really perfected the whole public bathroom sink bath. My head holds a complicated sketch of the city, sort of like the subway station maps, but based on public restrooms: parks, train stations, restaurants, movie theaters you can get into without too much trouble. Which ones have cherry soap, or bars of Ivory, or that weird useless antiseptic foaming spray. Gross. I hate the ones that have air dryers instead of paper towel dispensers, but paper towels are getting rarer and rarer.

Generally I try to wash up late at night, since there're fewer attendants to catch you and call security. In Grand Central last week, long after midnight, a cute guy came out of the stall and caught me rubbing hand soap into my armpit. He gave me a look, like, *gotcha*, but I just smiled and winked. He's the one who ought to be uncomfortable. He's just a tourist, after all.

Simon

Grand Central feels so opulent, with its high ceiling of turquoise and gold; when you step off the train you feel like it's all for you. I stalk toward the subway, feeling totally in control, and I swear to myself: *I'm not leaving this city until I get a blow job*. That resolve makes me proud: I've evolved, my shame is gone, I'm going after what I want, the future is mine. The high windows let in so much sun I could be riding the escalator up to heaven, and I'm glad to see there're no homeless people sleeping on newspaper on the steps and against the walls like when I came here as a kid in the '80s.

Solomon

On a newsstand I never noticed before there's a notice pinned up, from the Department of Health and Mental Hygiene, about an investigation of possible tainted heroin. *Male user reported intense and steadily increasing pain upon injection. Furthermore, he reported not experiencing his customary euphoria upon injection.* There's no number to call to report anyone, so I guess it's just a heads-up to the neighborhood junkies.

I keep moving, feeling like a ghost, uptown, downtown, as the day gets darker. A little girl outside a hotel screams like a seagull. Christmas songs blare outside a toy store. At Fifty-third Street, under an underpass, I watch water churned by the wind. Roosevelt Island's lights glint on the oily surface. A newer building, right on its edge, has huge condo-style windows in every apartment. They show ample views of the scene inside, but it's very bland: no sex I can see, just people washing dishes, watching television, mopping. Somewhere behind me, against one of the pillars that holds up the FDR, a guy getting a blow job comes with loud panting cries.

And then I'm on the train platform, waiting for the F, heading for Delancey Street, because it's Saturday afternoon, and there's always a punk-hardcore matinee at ABC No Rio. There's a woman on a pay phone, saying: "Your girlfriend is fucking lucky, because she was—I was drunk, and I had people in the car with me, and she would not be breathing right now."

Back at street level, feeling a little out of it for want of sleep, I come up to myself in the mirrored glass wall of a bank. I stop with a kind of shock, like bumping into a lost friend or some handsome stranger you're struck by and then realize is not a stranger at all. Who is this handsome devil? What is his life like? Where did he sleep last night?

Simon

When you walk in the door two things hit you: the sound of drumming and the smell of boy underarms. The building is old and rickety and the noise from the main room might shake it down. A staircase leading up looks like it will crumble under your weight, even if you're one of these super-skinny skateboard punks, but halfway up it two boys of totally reasonable girth stand talking, staring down at me with haughty looks that see clearly what a hick I am. The upper floors are dark and I can just barely make out a couple of rooms. I picture them as dank filthy spots perfect for random trysts, and I'm convinced the two boys standing so close on the narrow stair are plotting a bout of wanton sex up there. Overall the place has the feel of a small-scale tenement taken over by hooligans, the old ladies and immigrants all ejected and the space declared an autonomous state. The taller of the two boys catches me staring, and smiles, which turns him from bland to gorgeous. His teeth are perfect, his face is stubbled, he's got a sort of confidence I'm a million years from. It takes quite a mental effort to tear myself away from the sight of them and the thought of what they're going to do—although of course I know that they're probably just plotting their band's first show, or telling tall tales about a girl they both know.

I follow a hallway to the back and the noise gets louder. I try to read the graffiti covering the walls but it's too dark, only the odd phrase jumps out, nothing that makes sense, private jokes about bands and groupies and activist groups long since disbanded. In the doorway to the main space a pair of girls gossip, forced to the fringes by the seething sweating crowd I can hear and smell in there. "...Girls and fucked them at school; all I know is..." one of them is saying, but I don't linger, as much as I'm an eavesdropping addict. I keep moving because I'm picturing a crowd jam-packed with hot boys.

Which is exactly what I find. Boys in complicated leather coats, boys with Mohawks spiked up so high I swear they must have gotten hair extensions, boys shedding their winter jackets because the place is beastly hot with body heat. And the smell! It's like sticking your nose in the armpits of fifty guys at once, from the fresh and clean to the stale and disgusting, but even the gross side of it is sexy, intimate, naughty.

I push into the crowd and look around for a space to stand in. The band at the front is a bunch of Latino guys singing in Spanish, their sound a sort of punked up surf-rock—have I ever seen Latino guys at a punk-rock show?—and I'm conscious of two things at once. One: the band is really good, in an interesting, exciting sort of way that most of the punk I've been hearing back home, at the Valatie Elks Lodge and in Greg's basement, isn't. Two: I don't really care. The music's not touching me. The spark is gone: that telltale tingle I used to get at the raw, naked sound of power chords and screechy boy voices. What does this mean? Am I broken? Have I become a sellout, an autistic drone like everybody else—an adult?

I don't have a chance to be disturbed by this new development. I've never been surrounded by so many gorgeous young men before, and I repeat the resolution I made in Grand Central, make it a chant. I'm not leaving this city until I have sex with someone. At first I just say it to myself, but then I get bolder and start to mutter it, quietly, not that it matters, because the band is so loud people have to scream to be heard, and anyway, even if I were screaming it wouldn't matter, because no one here knows me, no one here would care.

"Is it always this crowded?" I ask a girl sitting behind the merchandise table.

"No," she says. "There's a lot of pretty big bands playing tonight. Plus it's a benefit for some kind of homeless organization, so, you know, lots of the political punk types turned out. The Stockyard Stoics are the headliners. Have you ever heard them?"

"No," I say.

"They're wonderful. You're going to love them. This your first time at ABC No Rio?"

"Yeah," I say, and offer her my hand. "I'm Simon."

"I'm Susie," she says, and shakes it. "You live in the city?"

"No, I live upstate."

"Oh."

"I gotta tell you, I've only been here like five minutes and this show knocks the pants off the rinky-dink punk shows my friends put on at the Elks Lodge and the Boys Club and stuff like that."

"Yeah, this place is the best."

Maybe punks are just much more resourceful down in the city, maybe they just have access to so much more stuff, but really, these kids have made themselves into stunning displays of punkness. Pants covered with band patches, jackets studded with giant spikes and chains and hooks, ears pierced with six safety pins, hair dyed to look like rainbow flags, punk-rock skinniness taken to disturbing extremes. If I lived in the city, I see, I'd have an eating disorder ten times worse than the one I have now.

Next to all this brilliant styling, the look I was so proud of when I double-checked it in my mom's full-length mirror looks downright dumb. Long underwear shirt, a Sex Pistols T-shirt, a pair of ripped jeans? What the hell is this, a Nirvana concert? Anybody who wears a T-shirt from a band you can get at Sam Goody's has got to be a loser. I see my chances of gagging on the cock of one of these guys dwindling fast.

From nervousness, I take out my camera and start taking pictures. The crowd is big enough that I can pretend I'm just taking general pictures when I'm actually zooming in on this hot boy or that one.

"Is this okay?" I ask the girl at the merch table, who for some reason I'm convinced is giving me the shark eye.

"Sure," she says. "You just gotta respect other people when they say they don't want to be photographed. We had this problem a couple of weeks ago—there was this old guy who used to come to all the shows, and he'd always bring this camera and take pictures of girls, and it was just totally creepy, so anyway, there was this band playing, and the singer's a girl, and he's right up front taking all these pictures, and the singer asked him to stop, and he wouldn't. So the collective had a meeting and decided he was going to be banned from future No Rio events."

"The collective?"

"Yeah, this place is run by a collective of volunteers who make all the major decisions. As long as you respect people and you're not a pervert, you ought to be fine."

"Who says I'm not a pervert?" I ask. "Although if I was, I'd be the sort that takes pictures of little boys, not little girls."

"Well, then, that's totally different. I am all for the sexual objectification of men. Way to fight patriarchy, dude!"

Solomon

I don't notice the boy I end up leaving with until my friend Kris leans over and says in my ear, "Who's your evil twin?" I look to where he's pointing and see a white guy about my height, but that's pretty much all we have in common.

"What are you talking about?" I ask Kris.

"He looks just like you."

"You need to stop smoking crack," I say, "it's doing horrible things to your brain."

"You two were separated at birth. You don't see it?"

"Not even a teeny bit."

"Okay. I'll talk you through it. Okay? Look: if you took away the corny half-assed I'm-too-young-for-stubble-but-I-think-it-makes-me-look-older stubble, and the butch skinhead haircut that screams "I'm a total faggot softie trying to look tough," and you took away the sparkling clean new clothes, and you gave the kid some lessons in style, well, there you are!"

"You're retarded."

"No I'm not. And now he's seen us staring, and he's staring back, but not at me! Because I don't look like I might be his long-lost twin brother."

"You're *so* retarded."

"Here he comes! Be still my beating heart."

The boy in the Sex Pistols T-shirt comes and stands near us and pretends to be trying to get a better view of the band. As the crowd shifts and writhes he inches closer, until he's standing as close to me as Kris.

"Aren't these boys just *divine*?" Kris asks him between songs.

"Yeah, I really like their sound."

"Who's talking about sound? I mean their *look*. I want to have sex with each and every one of them."

"I hear that," he says, and smiles goofily, looking back and forth between us both.

Simon

I ask the scruffier one if he wants to smoke, and he does. I offer one to his friend, who just waves his hand and says, "I have much better ways of killing myself, thanks."

"You come here a lot?" I ask on our way through the long narrow hall.

"I try to be here every Saturday. You know they do this every week. I love it. This is the best place in the city to see punk shows."

"I always wanted to see a show at CBGB."

"No you don't," he says. "That place is vile. Every single time I've been there, you hear fucking idiot guys in the bands saying all this homophobic and racist shit. It's horrible. This place does a great job of screening out that kind of shit."

"That's good."

"We can smoke out here," he says, pushing open a rusty old door to show a courtyard like some wrecked urban garden somewhere in England after the war.

"Nowhere to sit," I say, since the rain has soaked the benches and the tree stumps and the old ripped-up rocking chair.

"So who needs to sit," he says, smiling, and out of nowhere he's got a lit match cupped in his hand.

"I'm perfectly happy to stand," I say, and move close so he can light the cigarette in my mouth. When it's lit I don't step back.

"My friend Kris says you look like you could be my long-lost twin brother," he says. "Myself, I don't see it."

"Well, we're both totally gorgeous," I say. "So I can see how your friend would be confused." A slight smell of body odor wafts from his shirt, which is tattered in a way that might be intentional but might not, and his pants look like a strong wind would shred them, and his hair is lustrous from grease and pomade and the light drizzle still splashing onto us. I move a hand through it, rub my fingers against his scalp. "You have nicer hair than me."

"Aw, shucks," he says. "I use a special shampoo called sweat."

"Sexy."

Solomon

In spite of the general hardcore-boy look, which I usually hate, I'm totally crushing out on this kid. He's so clean-cut it cripples the hardcore vibe he's trying to get across. One of his feet is keeping the back door open, so a faint bit of light lets me see his features. He slouches, which somehow makes him look *taller*, like he's stooping down to keep from hitting his head. Yet he's almost exactly my height. Something tells me he bought his jeans special for tonight. From Abercrombie & Fitch. The light from the door shows me how flat his ass is. Me, I'm in shadow.

"Let the door shut," I say. "This courtyard is pretty neat at night."

When it clangs closed, I point up at the tenements that surround us. It's only eight PM, so there are lights in most of the windows. We see people moving around, living their lives.

"Wow," he says. "New York City is voyeur heaven."

"Where are you from?"

"I'm from a shitty little town upstate called Hudson. Horrible horrible place. I can't wait to graduate and go to college and get a bazillion-dollar job and be able to move to New York City."

"Sounds like a plan," I say.

My eyes have adjusted and I can just make out his face. He's looking at the shut door. "Will we be able to get back in?"

"Not sure."

"Come here," he says, and pulls me forward very gently by the face. With both hands on my chin. Our lips hit and he slides his hands around to the back of my head, rubs it, rolls his fingers all through my hair.

"I wish I'd showered before I came," I say.

"I'm glad you didn't," he says, his voice a whisper. "Your hair is so soft."

Simon

"You live around here?" I ask.

"No, not at all," he says, and chuckles. "I live in...Queens," and I swear he grimaces at the word.

"That's far?"

"It'd take us an hour and a half to get there by subway."

"By cab?"

"Just as long." He looks up at the bright windows of the buildings above us, and from my egotistical overactive-imagination perspective his eyes are moist—he's stricken at the thought of the chance he's missing.

"Why don't we get a hotel room?" I ask, my boldness making him blink. "I'm rolling in dough!"

"Are you kidding?" he asks. "Hotels are crazy expensive in New York!"

"You don't know of any good cheap fleabag motels?" I ask. "I've always had fantasies about that. What's the hotel where Sid Vicious killed his girlfriend?"

"I don't know any places like that," he says. "The only hotels I could even find are the touristy ones in Times Square."

"Well then. Let's go there. I'm telling you, I've been saving my pennies from the bookstore where I work, and I want to really live large on my one night in the big city."

"I can chip in some," he says, both hands sunk in his pockets.

"No, don't be silly," I say. "Listen, I've got three hundred dollars in my pocket and I don't want to leave this city with a single penny of it."

"I've never been to a hotel with anyone before," he says, folding his arms and looking at the ground. His cigarette is done.

"Me either. Exciting, no?"

Solomon

"What do you mean you've never been on the subway before? You mean you walked all the way from Grand Central Station?"

"Yeah."

"Oh my god! Why didn't you take the subway?"

"It scared me. I couldn't figure it out. I was afraid I'd get lost."

"Wow."

The rain has stopped completely. We walk toward the subway, heading for Times Square, heading for a hotel, and when we get off at Forty-second Street the Broadway shows must have just gotten out because the sidewalks are packed with people.

Families from all over the country, misty-eyed after *Cats* or *Phantom* or whatever. Big crowds around stage doors, waiting for the stars to come out and sign things.

Simon

The subway takes forever coming, and I'm already out of things to say to this weird slightly smelly city kid. On the wall is an ad against animal abuse, with Russell Simmons squatting to hug his pit bull. Under the dog someone wrote PIT BULLS ARE DUMB. Under that, someone said, SO ARE PEOPLE BUT THEY BOTH DESERVE RESPECT. Further down the same platform, someone tagged JIHAD DEATH across the endless forehead of the fat bald guy from *Seinfield.* On the train, two tired-looking black ladies talk about some rich rapper on the cover of a magazine one of them is holding. "And they're always talking about their big Rolexes. Talking about how they come from the street, how they grew up in the projects, how they still got people there. I don't care, long as I had anyone, third cousin, whatever, long as I had anyone in the projects you wouldn't see a hundred-thousand-dollar watch on my arm."

He takes me to a posh hotel in Times Square and we walk through the lobby and I'm feeling like a rich guy buying a hustler, I'm feeling on top of the world; I tell the lady at the desk I want a room "as high up as possible." And the room is almost two hundred dollars, and I pay in cash, and it's on the twenty-third floor, which doesn't sound so high, but when we get there and we look out the window it feels very high.

"Wow," he says, "I haven't stayed in a hotel room since I was a little little kid."

"Isn't it exciting? Hotels make me feel…important."

"I want to take a shower first," he murmurs, softly, when I wrap him in a bear hug and bury my face in his neck. "I stink."

"Don't worry about it," I say, my face burrowing down into his armpit. "I like it."

"No, I really need to take a shower. I haven't taken one in like forever."

"Be my guest," I say, magnanimously. Just in case he forgets he is. He's in there a long time and I spend most of it at the window, watching the crawl of cab lights and the barely-visible blips that are actually human beings, human lives as valid as my own. The hotel room's heat is up too high. When the shower stops I open the window and start to take off my clothes, listen to the noises he makes moving around in there. Faucet going on and off, towel scrubbing at his skin, toothbrush scratching at his teeth. Who carries a toothbrush around with them?

Solomon

He's standing by the window when I leave the bathroom. I go back to join him, and we kiss for a long time, wrapped in an increasingly complicated hug. The lights are all out except for in the bathroom, but the door there is mostly shut, and we're standing so that I can watch out the window. The city, throbbing like a giant organ. Nothing noble like a heart, more like a huge heap of intestines. Or some sick animal, dying slowly. Or the ocean.

In a hotel you know you belong. It's like an apartment: money has changed hands, and money gives you legitimacy. When you're sleeping on someone's floor the dark outside is stronger, and louder. You're only there by the grace of a courtesy that might vanish at any moment. And then where would you be?

Simon

Since I was thirteen I've fantasized about sucking my own dick, and this must be sort of what it feels like. His head bobs up and down and in the poor light from the half-shut bathroom door he looks just like me. What an egotistical little son of a bitch I am!

Solomon

As happy as I am, I have a hard time sleeping, and when I do fall asleep I keep waking up. I meditate on the lovely sight of his back, his neck, lit by light from the street. But when I try to curl up against him he twitches, jerks himself away. I wish I could go get my notebook out of my backpack. The stubble on his cheek, like the grain in an old black-and-white flick, jerks and jumps as he sleeps.

Simon

In Grand Central I buy coffee, and two Danishes, because I'm just that hungry and just that rich, and go down a broad marble staircase built for me in the age of the Rockefellers and the Morgans, and my train is waiting, the first train out of the station that morning, and it's totally empty.

When we chug out from underground it's still dark out, and we pass through Spanish Harlem and then Harlem Proper and then we cross the river and we're in the Bronx, and lights are glimmering in buildings and the highways are already starting to clog with early-morning commuters. I sip my expensive coffee, which has a funny aftertaste, vaguely interested in all the poverty the darkness is hiding.

Soon we're out of the city limits and it's starting to get brighter out. The river rolls by like a movie being shown for me alone, like this whole beautiful countryside just coming awake was built for my amusement. Trains pass mine, heading south, full of men in business suits, and those men used to scare me, but not anymore. After last night I see I'll end up with them, with the same power and responsibilities, the same excessive cologne, the same demons, the same conviction that absolutely anything I want will be mine, only I'll be *out*, and I'll have more sex than any man can handle, and life will be wonderful.

We pull into Poughkeepsie and it's only seven AM. The air is damp and hot and the cold metal of the stairway railing shocks me when I put my hand to it: I lean my face against it and shiver. I parked three blocks from the station, and there's a definite tune emanating from my lips as I stroll through the warm summer air. When I get back to my car, I notice that my hands smell like blood from the iron railing.

Solomon

It's one of those days where I've been walking a couple hundred blocks and the rhythm of it takes over, and I'm not even thinking anymore. After my shower last night, after sex last night, my thighs aren't chafed and achy and my feet aren't soaked and sore. It's like the stage past frostbite, when you stop feeling the cold, just before you die.

Dark-gray snow is piled up over my head in spots, in huge banks along the curb. Not to be too melodramatic about things, but I'm just starting to feel like one of those Antarctic explorers who died trying to find a totally meaningless tiny patch of barren frozen tundra indistinguishable from thousands of miles of identical barren frozen tundra. The bottom of the world. A new Gap is going up on One Hundred Twenty-fifth, and in the windows giant posters totally inappropriate for the season say COMING SOON! and show healthy suburban white boys playing soccer in rugby shirts and jeans. I'm very happy to find that this particular type, which used to turn me on because it stimulated my jealousy, no longer interests me.

On One Hundred Twenty-third Street, a block west of Marcus Garvey Park, there's a stoop crowded with men. I make eye contact with one when I pass: a handsome, older man, but down in the dumps, with a snotty nose and dirty clothes. Crackhead eyes. It's not until I've turned the corner that the little smile he gave me hits home: it was Earl's smile. Earl, first guy I slept with after leaving home. I want to turn back but don't dare, wouldn't know what to say. *Sorry to hear you lost your place and are back on the streets?* Trying to think of how long it's been since the last time I saw him makes me realize how long I've been out myself.

ONE OF THE GUYS

Jameson Currier

"Cool," Jonathan answered when Tavo had laid out the plans for their evening after work: drinks, dinner, clubbing. He nodded and added another "Cool" and felt his nervousness and youthfulness showing, though Tavo was already on the way back to his cubicle and had not witnessed Jonathan's deterioration into discomfort. Jonathan was twenty-five and had been working at the accounting firm for less than a year, though he was still treated like a young college intern fresh from Long Island. Everyone in the company had a little too much information and advice for him, mixed in with a fake friendliness and a phony interest in his personal life, believing that he was on course for a management position because of his class ranking and an accelerated master's degree in finance. But Tavo was also the first person to suggest that Jonathan was a bit too serious and naïve in the workplace, which is why Jonathan wanted to be more like Tavo: casual, sexy, and sought after.

Tavo (short for Gustavo) was six years older than Jonathan

and wore his physique like a tight, flashy uniform. A corporate casual-attire dress code had been adopted by the firm shortly before Jonathan began working in the office, and Tavo had a preference for snug khaki pants that displayed his generous buns and crotch, and short-sleeved polo shirts that showed off his extravagant biceps and wisps of black underarm hair, and, if you were lucky and looking (which most everyone was), a peek of the chain link tattoo that circled his upper arm when he stretched to reach for a pencil or a disc. Nina, the fiftysomething departmental secretary, had a dozen nicknames she taunted and teased Tavo with every time he passed by her desk (even though she knew it was corporately unethical for her to do so), from "Big Boy" to "Hot Buns" to "Sexy Thang" and "Mr. Man."

Tavo worked with the IT department, short for Internet Technologies or I've got IT (and you don't), though it was uncertain exactly what he did when he would show up and fumble on the computer keyboard at a workstation and ask for user passwords. He had an arrogant attitude, never explaining what he was searching for or what he had discovered, which no one seemed to mind because his visit was treated as special as a personal appearance by a porn star; even the managers found him a breath of fresh air, or, for that matter, a breath of what the real world could be like outside their offices and with a body like that and with an assortment of sexual partners waiting in a long line to be picked out and taken home. In the mornings before his shift started Tavo could be seen hanging around outside the building on the sidewalk in front of the lobby entrance talking with his buddies who smoked, other slim, narrow-waisted spiky-haired young guys who also worked in IT and made it look like they were part of a private clique. At lunchtime they all sat together at the center table in the cafeteria so that it was impossible to overlook them. It was rumored that Tavo and his buddies would probably fuck anything that walked into the room at the right time, though Jonathan knew that Tavo was a bit more discriminating than his reputation belied. He had a weakness for short, tightly built Latino guys just like himself. Jonathan had learned about Tavo's preferences after a casual remark in the men's room one morning when Tavo, unshaved and groggy (but still sexy, magnificently so) and standing in front of the sinks and the mirror, confessed his hangover and described the trick from the night before who had kept him up and happy and intoxicated. There followed other private remarks from Tavo about his so-called not-really-gay but very-gay life—such as a list of titles of his favorite DJ remixes or a detailed description of the interior of a house in the Pines or a deliberation of the best after-parties on Pride weekend—all of which often left Jonathan uncertain as to whether they were intended to be repeated to the rest of the office staff.

Ironically, Jonathan was not as closeted and secretive about his sexual preference as Tavo and his buddies were. He was openly gay, though he was uncertain what that meant exactly at the moment, since he was not an activist or a volunteer (or, he sometimes joked, a recruiter for the "gay agenda") and he seldom went to the bars and clubs and had not had a boyfriend since his junior year in college, the year he came out. Still, Jonathan kept up with "the culture," picking up the local gay bar rags and newspapers at his video store, visiting the library at the gay and lesbian community center in the Village, and chatting up Nina or one of the other secretaries about their favorite movies, actors, music videos, and singers.

Jonathan lived in a basement apartment of his parents' house in Melville, commuting on the Long Island Rail Road every morning into Manhattan and walking the fifteen-plus blocks to the firm's midtown address. His dream was to meet a guy, the *right* guy, and move in together, sharing a life of Broadway musicals, dance clubs, and gallery openings. For now, he kept his personal life simple and adaptable, available to hang out with a potential boyfriend or one or two of his friends from school who still lived in the neighborhood, or, when necessary, spend face time with his family.

Lian was standing beside Tavo when Jonathan found him in the lobby after work. Jonathan hadn't known that Lian would be joining them and was slightly disappointed because he had wanted Tavo to himself for the night (with the hope that Tavo might want to turn their outing into something more intimate and sexual). But Jonathan was also relieved when Tavo told him that they were stopping by Lian's apartment first; Lian's presence would keep Tavo's focus away from Jonathan's inexperience and apprehension.

Lian was a head taller than Tavo and Jonathan, dark haired, blue eyed, with an unmemorable face until you'd had a chance to study it. Then he was suddenly the most handsome man in the room—square jawed with a slender nose, high cheekbones, a deep chesty voice with a hint of a British accent, and an Adam's apple that seemed to maintain its own erection. Unlike Tavo, with his stocky, flashy power, Lian was a quiet loner—the kind of guy out for a jog in Central Park or along the West Side Highway on a rainy Saturday morning instead of working out with a group of friends at the gym. Lian's work as a programmer seldom took him far from his desk, which was why he was infrequently noticed or remembered. But it was clear to Jonathan that if everyone's attention revolved around Tavo, Tavo's attention orbited Lian.

Jonathan followed behind the pair like a puppy dog, sidestepping the pedestrians left in their wake as they walked to the subway. On the downtown platform waiting for the train, Tavo bounced on the heels of his feet as if he were listening to a dance tune; Lian stood beside him aloof but amused. Jonathan tried to look like he belonged but felt more like a voyeur, or an interloper, or worse, like he had felt in high school, like an outcast around the more popular guys.

Lian lived in a building on West Nineteenth Street, not far from the bar where Tavo had suggested they go for drinks before dinner. While they waited for the building elevator to arrive, Jonathan glanced at the notices of missing dogs and undelivered packages, and the business cards of photographers, editors, computer geeks and masseurs posted on a bulletin board in the lobby, wishing he were part of this everyday urban life. Lian's apartment was on the fifth floor, a one bedroom converted into two, with a big navy blue sofa opposite the wall where the sink and stove were located in the area designed to serve as the kitchen. The décor was rather nonexistent, except for a framed poster of a leaping dolphin that looked like it belonged in a dorm room instead of on the wall of a gay man's apartment in Chelsea. Inside, Tavo asked Lian when his roommate Philip would be home and Lian answered with a choppy, "Soon. But I got something till then."

Jonathan sat on the couch, took in a deep, nervous breath and told himself he could do whatever Tavo could do; and asked what music Tavo was looking for in a shelf of CDs. "Black Party mix," Tavo answered. "Dude burned it special."

Tavo found the CD and slipped it into Lian's stereo system. A heavy bass soon vibrated the walls and floor and Jonathan's shoes. Jonathan sat and watched Tavo dance with himself until Lian returned to the room with a joint. Jonathan relaxed. *Just pot.* Something he had done before without any problem. He took a toke when Tavo passed it to him and followed them into Lian's bedroom to check out something Lian was downloading onto his computer. It was a video clip of a man's cock, reported to be part of a longer sex tape made of a certain rising male celebrity. Jonathan had already seen it—he'd downloaded it himself two nights before after he had read about it in a magazine he had found at the grocery store—and he said, "Sorta unfair, isn't it? A guy that good-looking with such a big cock."

Lian nodded and laughed and said, "As long as he shares it."

Tavo chuckled and it made Jonathan feel like he belonged, like he was one of the guys. Jonathan sat on the edge of Lian's bed beside Tavo, and they passed the joint between them until it was done.

Lian flipped on the television in the bedroom, the dance music still on the stereo in the other room, and they sat and watched an entertainment news program recap highlights of celebrity blunders. Tavo disappeared and returned with a bag of taco chips and Lian said, "We can order Chinese. Philip likes Moo Shu."

Jonathan was only slightly depressed. He had wanted to go to one of the trendy Eighth Avenue restaurants—Tavo had even suggested a few of his favorites—to be part of a flashy gay crowd, but he was also glad there was a cheaper alternative—his paycheck did not seem to be stretching the way he thought it should. The pot had made him hungry and he greedily took a handful of taco chips from the bag Tavo was holding, and said, "I love plum sauce."

Tavo and Lian both gave him a confused look. "The plum sauce that goes on the pancake when you order Moo Shu Pork," he added.

They seemed to understand and nodded. They watched some more television and during a commercial break Lian found a menu for a Chinese restaurant. Tavo disappeared and reappeared with beers and Jonathan drank more than half the bottle at once, unaware till then of how thirsty he had become. He felt a happy, light-headed bliss now and he found it difficult to hold back his smiling. He thought Tavo and Lian were the greatest friends he could ever find. Jonathan held the menu in his lap and Tavo and Lian huddled close around him, and he could smell their warm salty breath and syrupy antiperspirant. Tavo said he wanted something with rice noodles, "the really sticky white kind," which made Lian laugh and say he didn't have a take-out menu for Thai food, but they could probably find something white and sticky if they tried.

Jonathan let the innuendo waft over him, as if he were as naïve as his new friends believed he was, and he asked them if they liked "pot stickers." Again, they didn't seem to understand what he said, so he pointed to the menu and said, "Dumplings. Fried dumplings."

They both smiled and nodded and when their attention seemed to drift away from the menu and back to the television, Jonathan said that he would be glad to order the Chinese food. His gesture went unanswered, which Jonathan took as a passive-aggressive manner of confirmation, and going into the kitchen area, he turned off the stereo and found the phone beside the sofa and ordered dumplings, Singapore Mei Fun (with rice noodles for Tavo), General Tso's Chicken (for Lian), and Moo Shu Pork and Chicken (for himself and Lian's roommate since he was unable to remember if Lian had said that Philip liked pork or chicken best).

When he had hung up, he realized he was feeling dehydrated and he searched through the kitchen cabinets for a glass, but found none. He turned on the faucet at the sink and slipped his mouth into the flow of water and swallowed till he felt full. The water was cold against the back of his throat and he wiped his mouth and chin with the sleeve of his dress shirt. He wished he had known beforehand that Tavo had wanted to do something this evening; he would have dressed more casual, or, rather, not have worn his best work shirt and dress pants to party in.

Back in the bedroom Tavo and Lian were lying on the bed still watching television. Jonathan stood and watched the program—now one of those nature shows about kangaroos in Australia (one of them must have changed the channel)—and thought how envious everyone at work would be of him, being in a bedroom with Tavo even though nothing was happening (or looking like it would happen). When the buzzer rang a few minutes later, Jonathan went into the kitchen area and located the buzzer on the wall and let the delivery boy inside the building.

While he waited, Jonathan checked the money in his wallet—he had enough to cover the delivery and he could collect payment from the guys at work the next day if they didn't ante up when the food arrived. He stood by the door for a few minutes and waited, then grew restless and sat on the sofa and flipped through a magazine and read the escort ads in the back. He'd lost track of time—a good ten minutes—when there was a knock at the door. Jonathan paid and tipped the delivery boy—the boy muttered something to Jonathan, which he took to be about the sluggishness of the elevator—and then Jonathan emptied the bags on the small counter in the kitchen. He walked into the bedroom and said, "Food's here." Tavo and Lian both gave him blank looks, as if they had forgotten Jonathan was even in the apartment. The bag of taco chips between them was empty.

Then suddenly, as if someone had flipped a switch, they sprung up from the bed and were in the kitchen, going through the cartons of food. Tavo sat cross-legged on the floor and ate with chopsticks, as if it were the most natural thing to do. Lian perched on the side arm of the couch and used a fork, eating directly from the container. Jonathan stood at the counter and used a paper plate to spread out the plum sauce onto his pancake and roll up his Moo Shu into something that resembled a burrito. Someone had turned the stereo back on (or Jonathan thought that perhaps he had only turned down the volume when he had used the phone; it seemed like such a long time ago and he couldn't even remember walking into the apartment). The music thumped and vibrated and kept each of them occupied and silent. While they were eating the front door unlocked and Lian's roommate Philip walked in, smartly dressed in a gray business suit, white shirt, and yellow-patterned tie.

"Party time!" Philip said above the heavy bass beat, when he saw Lian and Tavo eating. He nodded at Jonathan and said, "Hey," and Jonathan responded likewise. Philip was Tavo's height, but had Lian's slender, gentleman's build, though the similarity ended there. Philip had a swarthy five o'clock shadow, tiny black eyes, a wide lower jaw and thick red lips that opened to a bright smile of oversized teeth that appeared almost cartoonish. It was immediately apparent (to Jonathan, at least) that the alpha male figure of the group had arrived and whatever fun Tavo had been planning for them was now ready to begin.

"Looks like I got to catch up with you guys," Philip said, smirking so widely that it seemed almost unnatural. He disappeared into the room behind the navy sofa—a living room that had been walled over to create a second bedroom in the apartment. He emerged a few minutes later dressed in jeans and an olive green T-shirt. On the kitchen counter he tapped out the contents of a vial onto a paper plate and used a rolled-up dollar bill to snort a fine white powder up his nostrils. He turned to the guys and said, "Want a hit?"

Tavo leapt up off the floor and took a quick hit up one nostril, then dipped a fingertip into the powder and rubbed it into his gums. Lian waved his fork and said, "Later," which Jonathan felt grateful for because it allowed him to say the same thing.

Philip stood at the counter and took a few bites of Moo Shu directly from the container, then asked if anyone wanted a drink. Again Tavo leapt up off the floor and said, "Let's try that flavored vodka."

Jonathan watched Philip pull down glasses from the cabinet—aware and amazed at how he had overlooked them earlier in his quest for a glass—and set about mixing a pepper-flavored vodka with cranberry juice and ice for everyone. The finished product was strangely tart and spicy when Jonathan tasted it (and seemed to hover in a clog of phlegm at the back of his throat). Tavo had finished his Mei Fun and had bagged it up and tossed it into a plastic trash bag (at Philip's insistence; they had seen a mouse in the apartment the previous week). Jonathan bagged up his and Lian's containers while Tavo danced and showed off his rhythm, telling the guys that there was a special "dog tag" night at a club in the East Village. Jonathan had no idea what a "dog tag" night was, and wasn't about to ask. The beer and the joint and the cocktail had worked their magic and he was feeling giddy and bloated and he went into the bathroom at the side of the kitchen and took a long piss. At the sink he rinsed his hands and face and wiped them dry on a towel, breathing in as much odor as he could detect, trying to determine if it belonged to Lian or Philip. Jonathan now felt not only happy, but safe and lucky and indestructible. He felt like they would all be friends forever. Back in the kitchen, Philip had fixed Jonathan another drink and when he handed it to Jonathan, he said, "You've got great lips."

The compliment made Jonathan smile—no one had ever said that to him—and before he knew it (and before he could take the drink from Philip) Philip had pressed his mouth against Jonathan's face, swallowing his lips into a wide, wet and sloppy, tongue-twisting kiss. Jonathan's reaction was a tension that flared up his spine and branched out across his shoulders, a tension that he could not release.

Philip pulled away and said, "Relax, baby. I bet I've got something you want to try." Jonathan thought Philip was referring to his cock. Or a dildo or a sex toy. And that he could easily dismiss—or accept—whatever sexual game was afoot, though he had no desire to be a "rotten sport" about any of it.

Philip arched his eyebrows, as if he were a game show host about to reveal the correct answer, and disappeared into the second bedroom. When he returned he held up for Jonathan to see a tiny white pill between his thumb and finger and said, "This will make you feel mighty fine."

Jonathan was all set to ask what it was—or what it would do—when Philip grandly placed the pill on the tip of his own tongue. Philip waved his tongue suggestively back and forth at Jonathan—which made Jonathan smile uneasily. Philip pulled Jonathan back into another big, wide, sloppy kiss and the pill was suddenly in Jonathan's mouth. By the time Jonathan had realized what had happened and was trying to prevent himself from swallowing it, the pill had dissolved in his mouth.

"What was that?" Jonathan asked nervously.

"Just a little fun," Philip said. "You probably won't feel a thing."

Tavo had danced back into the room and was saying, "Gimme, gimme," to Philip. Philip performed the same grand ritual with Tavo, placing another pill on the tip of his tongue and pulling Tavo into a deep, mouthy kiss. Jonathan relaxed a bit, watching Tavo accept the drug. Again he thought that if Tavo was doing it, then he could handle whatever effects the drug might have.

"Now you do it," Philip said to Jonathan, holding up another pill between his fingers. "For Lian."

How could he resist? Jonathan had been eyeing Lian's behavior since they had left the office, trying to interpret his body language to see if he had any interest in him. If Jonathan had to make a decision between Tavo and Lian—one or the other—he would be reluctant to give up Tavo, but Lian was closer to being the man of his dreams—tall, handsome, mysterious, full of potential and possibilities. Tavo was really a boy with a man's muscles. Now there was an opportunity to kiss Lian—when might that ever happen again?—and it would only bring them closer, make Jonathan feel like he was part of a special, private boys' club.

Philip grandly put the pill on the end of Jonathan's tongue. Lian clasped his hand at the back of Jonathan's neck. Jonathan leaned his head up and stood on his tiptoes as Lian swooped in to kiss him. Jonathan let his mouth remain open as long as Lian wanted to be there. Lian's hand tightened around the back of Jonathan's neck and sent the blood rushing dizzily around Jonathan's body. Then Lian's free hand cupped Jonathan's back and he slid it down and underneath his belt and underwear, cupping the flesh of Jonathan's buttock. Jonathan could not prevent his erection and Lian's hand dug further down his pants, curving further and further till his fingers reached the warm sack of Jonathan's balls. Jonathan felt himself falling, felt Lian catching him, or holding him up, or lifting him up in the air. He was both thrilled and alarmed by his fear and desire.

Everything seemed to decompose from that moment—disconnect and deconstruct and disengage. He was aware of Lian's aggressiveness continuing as they continued to kiss—his other hand struggling to touch the flesh of Jonathan's chest, then moving down to cup his straining crotch. Lian unzipped Jonathan's fly and reached inside, stroking his cock and kneading his balls from this angle, then fell to his knees and took Jonathan's cock into his throat.

Jonathan's tension evaporated—he felt a balloon of pleasure behind his eyes—the navy blue sofa turning shades lighter, the dolphin on the wall leaping higher, the wood of the kitchen cabinets bleaching into the white wall. Tavo moved in and began kissing Jonathan—yes, kissing him, *Jonathan*—who in the office would ever believe this moment?—Tavo *and* Lian—while Lian was now forcefully sliding his lips and fingers across Jonathan's cock. Jonathan's orgasm came in a swift oh-my-gosh moment—he found a Herculean strength to push Lian slightly away as he shot over his shoulder and Tavo turned his head and watched the spectacle with a light laugh.

"Told you he'd be a quick one," Lian said to Tavo, as if there had been a bet in place between the two about how quickly Jonathan would come. Jonathan could not remember his reaction; it seemed to fall away, or fall into Philip's mouth. Now it was Philip who was moving in front of him, groping him. Then they were on the couch, then elsewhere, laughing on the floor, removing their socks—they felt as heavy as dictionaries or encyclopedias or almanacs or Bibles or phone books. Heavy. Burdens. They made Jonathan feel better when they were off.

Then they were in another place—against the wall—then together, on a bed. All of them. All four of them. On the bed. *In* bed. *Together*.

Jonathan returned to consciousness after a dream about trying to swim out of a whirlpool, keeping his head above water. The lights in the bedroom were on and he blinked them into awareness as if his eyes had been full of water. The music was still playing on the stereo in the other room, the heavy beat now traveling through the floorboards and up the wooden frame of the bed. Philip was asleep beside him, his black pebbly chin stretched out against the mattress as if he were a dog searching for air. Jonathan closed his eyes, felt himself rising off the bed as if pulled by a magician's showy gesture, and he fluttered his eyes open again. The orbiting and swirling continued and Jonathan tried to shake away the nausea from his stomach. His throat was dry. His lips were gummy. He sat up and placed a foot against the floor, wrapped his hands around his forehead to stop the spinning. Upright, he propped himself against a closet door, the music now louder and softer, the spinning continuing like he was inside a blender. He felt the chill of the floor at the heel of his foot and the cold traveled up his bare body and settled into his shoulders. Philip was cocooned in a sheet. Jonathan reached across the bed and lifted the olive green T-shirt off the blanket where it was curled up like an odd-colored cat and put it on.

As he passed the door of Lian's bedroom, he saw Tavo sleeping facedown on the mattress, his hairy ass perched in the air as if he was awaiting penetration. Lian was curled on his side in a fetal position with a pillow between his legs. Jonathan made his way to the bathroom and turned on the faucets and waited for the warm water to wash into the sink. He rinsed and dried his face, ran his mouth beneath the faucet and a cooler flow of water. He did not leave the bathroom. The spinning continued. He tried to steady himself by looking at a clock on the bathroom wall and calculating if he might still have a chance to catch a train back to Long Island. He could sleep on the commute. He'd feel better elsewhere. At home. Not here.

He found his clothes on the floor in front of the navy sofa. He slipped on his pants and dress shirt, tucked his socks in his pockets and slowly laced up his shoes, as if he were already an old man with arthritis. His head continued its pounding and he tried not to exert himself, hoping to keep the pain manageable.

He left the apartment, moving slowly and gently closing the door behind him. He waited a few minutes for the elevator with his hand pressed against the wall and his head lowered, and then he gave up, descending five flights of stairs that seemed more like fifty. It was dark outside but the air was cool and fresh.

An ambulance picked him up an hour later. He was lying on the pavement outside a restaurant on Eighth Avenue. A policeman had arrived, believing Jonathan was dead. "I took something," Jonathan whispered as he was lifted onto a stretcher.

The next morning he found himself in the hallway of a hospital on the East Side with an IV hooked to his arm. He slept until a policeman arrived to question him about what drugs he had taken and where he had gotten them. Jonathan mentioned nothing about Philip or Tavo or Lian, only that he had gone to a party at an apartment and had taken a pill. He told the officer that he could not remember where the apartment was located. His wallet and watch were missing and he reported them stolen. He felt pains in his stomach, his head, and oddly, in the heel of his left foot.

A few hours later, when his body fluids were stable, Jonathan was released because of overcrowding in the emergency room. He walked across town to his office building and took the elevator to his floor. He nodded at Nina as he passed her desk and went directly down the hall to the men's restroom. He stood in front of the mirror and rinsed his face and patted down his hair. He took some warm water and gargled and used a fingertip as a toothbrush and scraped some of the grime from his teeth.

As he was tucking his shirt into his pants—and noticing the olive green T-shirt he was wearing underneath—Tavo walked into the men's room. He looked showered and clean and refreshed. He had even shaved. "Fun night," he said to Jonathan. "Enjoy yourself?"

"Sure did," Jonathan answered. "Let's do it again soon."

TINY GOLDEN KERNEL

Lee Houck

When I was little, my mother told me that inside everyone, at the absolute center of us, there is a tiny golden kernel, our essence distilled down to something pure, elemental, something very close to a soul. She told me that radiating from this small kernel are thousands of vaporous strings, impossibly thin, like the rippling pink licks that float inside a plasma globe. And those strings hold us all intact like a magic anchor; tied with miniscule square knots to our organs, our bones, our skin, they pull our bodies back toward that absolute center, toward that precious kernel, like our own unique gravity.

I used to stand in the middle of my bedroom, arms splayed out, looking at my naked body in the mirror, wearing the cheap X-ray glasses I'd mail-ordered out of the back of a comic book, trying to see through my flesh, trying to locate that shining golden center. I would squeeze my eyes closed for a minute and open them quickly, as if to sneak up on the real me. I would curl into a ball under the sheets, the bedroom dark, the curtains closed and the lamp turned off, expecting the light from that kernel to shine out from my insides, a flickering orange glow, like a faraway candle.

But as I got older, passing involuntarily through the summers as a horny, lanky teenager, somehow those pink strings began to stretch and break. Imagine your body growing larger, inflated, ballooning out—imagine time as physical distance—your edges moving ever further away from the core that holds you together.

It had never occurred to me that I could make money doing what I did. Sleeping with men wasn't a pastime, it wasn't a hobby. It was who I was. Or it was the way I figured out who I was. Sex was how I learned to read myself. It was where I learned to disappear into the other side of the known world, sink into that flat place. It allowed me access to my hidden self, that unknown person that comes scratching its way to the surface, unexpectedly. It unlocks a space, a landscape, a perpetual wind.

The first time I got paid for sex, it was an accident. I had picked someone up, or maybe he had picked me up—however that mutual glancing is decided. He was rich (so he said) and happily married (so he also said,) and he poised his pen over his checkbook after I had finished. "One hundred dollars," he mumbled, as if he were speaking to nobody in particular—and at the time, I didn't know what kind of money I was worth. I was still breathing hard, my temples moist with sweat. He wrote it out, tearing along the perforated line, a clean, satisfying sound. And I took it, foolishly I know now—who takes checks? But he stuck a twenty in my pocket and asked if I'd come back in two weeks. So for almost a year there were one or two appointments a month. One time we fucked on the sofa, and I accidentally knocked a lamp off the end table. I didn't stop—he loved it—and he said he'd blame it on the maid.

I got better at it. People traded my number around.

Men called with hushed voices, confused when one of my parents answered the phone, and I became wary and anxious—afraid of being caught, I suppose—each time it rang. There were so many hang-ups that they considered removing the line entirely. But more than anything else, more than the phone calls, the wads of cash lying suspiciously around my bedroom, my coming and going at all hours, what really became the central issue—or, I know now, what *had always been* the central issue—were the growing differences in what we wanted from the world. It was the surfacing of a fundamental alienation that had been there all along—the reality of our lives suddenly made visible.

"Why don't you want what we want?" my mother actually asked.

My parents were full of disappointments. With me, of course, but with their own lives, too. And my desire for something more meaningful (at least meaningful to me) in this life than fifty-minute church services and potluck dinners with chitchatting strangers, was somehow taken personally.

We tried to "make it easier on everyone." Their words, not mine. We had gone through the usual steps. First, a promise to be where I said I would be (never mind that they didn't *really* want to know where I was, and so I lied to save them from it) and to be home at "a reasonable hour," though it was unclear what exactly that meant. Second, my own separate, side entrance to the house—that sort of controlled freedom. They were slowly kicking me out, pointing out along the way that "you're only doing this to yourself."

They stopped speaking to me unless it was absolutely necessary, preferring instead to communicate through small notes stuck to the kitchen counter, appearing from nowhere, as if left by hotel housekeeping. Even the notes were stilted and shallow, cryptic, as if language was strange to them, as if they simply lacked the words. *Your father has gone for a few days.* (Gone to *where*, I thought.) *Turn off the pot roast when you wake up.* And sometimes, as if it were her punishment: *We love you.*

All my mother wanted was for me to be happy—whatever that means—and all my father wanted was to think about his queer son as little as possible.

All I ever wanted was someone who would stay.

I bought a train ticket to New York City, and the trip felt like a new beginning—the inauguration of an altered, unaccustomed life. I wondered what the other people on the train were trying to get away from. Because that's what trains were to me then—escape—and that's how everything looked to me, speeding across the land. Nameless places, small Virginia and North Carolina towns that exist for what purpose? As we got closer, people got more excited. Even at three and four in the morning, reading lamps were on, people were whispering to each other, quietly laughing.

That memory is very clear to me, those moments locked inside the train with strangers. My head documents those anonymous moments in more detail, in an easily retrievable, up-front kind of way. So many private moments in the company of men who want, among other things, to get off.

When I arrived in New York it was just past dawn, a quiet Sunday morning. I grabbed my bags and climbed up the stairs stained with decades of city muck, emerging. There was a specific quiet, an uncomplicated city sound. And I was alive, nauseous with sleep deprivation, but buzzing with presence, newness. Sometimes, if you're lucky enough to be up at that hour, that early Sunday sunrise, you get to see everything frozen in a loose opaque haze, like everything is coated in a lustrous numbing powder. The buildings here are huge, leaping out of the ground.

Billboards as tall as buildings. Radio towers on top of buildings. Everything wants to rocket-launch itself into the sky. Escape the concrete. Fire off, soar away.

I asked around, found out where people like me hung out. Which bars, which corners, where we could stand without being chased off. There are plenty of places. Of course, I never need to do that now; I'm busy enough with repeats. In fact, the messages I got today—three calls from people who want to get fucked—mean potentially six hundred easy dollars (assuming I can get hard enough to fuck three people in one afternoon).

And then there's Aiden. I don't even know what he does when I'm not around: job, hobbies, TV watching—all the seemingly banal details that make up a life. My friend Jaron says I'm in love. I believe that I could be—in the way that Jaron means it. The way love can be a temporary insanity, the kind of madness that sounds like your only defense in a courtroom. "I'm sorry your honor, I didn't know what the hell I was doing."

Jaron says I'm stuck, frozen with ten thousand options in front of me, and therefore choosing none. I believe him. Or I want to believe him. But am I capable of that? Capable of wanting, finding and successfully sustaining a love of that warm and fuzzy universal magnitude? It's an interesting word to use: *capable.* As if it were a dexterity that could be learned, practiced and executed, like a sport or a skill.

Aiden does cause strange sensations, things that I haven't felt before. Stirring things deep in my stomach, a whirring of distant noises in my head. A room full of faces, whispering rumors that may or may not be true. The pressing of personalities against glass.

Can you pinpoint when this sort of thing happens? Can you pry through the layers of skin and blood and isolate that precious golden kernel, protect it, save it, let it glow brilliantly inside you? Can you press your finger on a moment, holding it down, and say: Here—this is where it all changed?

I still hear my mother asking that question, not in my dreams exactly, maybe it even comes from inside me—"Why don't you want what we want?" I think she thought I might have the answer.

TAMING THE TREES

Jeff Mann

The fucking chain saw starts up just after dawn. I push my head-throb deeper into the flannel sheets for a few minutes—too many Manhattans last night. Then the snarl of a second chain saw joins the first—talk about contrapuntal cacophony—and I drag my ass out of bed. Jerking on a pair of boxer briefs, I stride to the window overlooking the street. There are six Asplundh workers today, one of them riding his little extendable basket into the air so as to better decapitate the maples along Seventh Street. I curse, scratch my beard, and wish I had a shotgun.

Another day of arboreal butchery in this small-town neighborhood. Heaven fucking forfend the trees would run a little wild. Our local "vegetation managers," as they call themselves, have been bringing down maple and hemlock limbs all week. In order to protect the power lines, that's what they'd say. I think they just enjoy making a mess. I think they like the way the trees look after they're done, like cripples, amputees, unlucky young soldiers back from that idiotic war overseas. "Taming the trees," that's what my father wryly calls it. Teaching the wild and the free a lesson. Diminishing, domesticating, civilizing.

What my last boyfriend tried to do to me, the bossy bastard. Then I got another tattoo, filling up my entire left shoulder with tribal swirls. He threw a fit, I threw him out. Now I'm living alone again, what world's left to me is budding with mid-March, hyacinths in the front beds are about to pop, and I'm watching the maples' equivalents of biceps, triceps, fingers, and hands being sawed off.

I can't help but commiserate. These days my hands are consigned to making love not to men but to computer keyboards.

Of course, even in the midst of my anger, part of me's checking out the chain saw wielders to see if any are hot. Most of today's workers are middle-aged guys like me, ones I'd just as soon shoot in the knees, considering how deftly and brutally they're ruining the streetscape. Only one member of the tree-butchers looks fuckable—a brawny country boy with a thick black goatee, baseball cap, big shoulders, flannel shirt, down vest, grimy jeans, and muddy work boots.

Bear cub. The way I used to look twenty-five years ago. The kind of man I want the most—younger, hotter versions of myself—and, now that I'm fifty, the kind of man I haven't had for years and am not liable to land again.

Here in the mountains, men who look like that are almost always straight. Hell, even if the boy out the window were gay, how likely is it that he'd want a silver-bearded daddy bear like me to tie him up? He'd most likely want a man his own age, and he'd most likely want vanilla sex. The laws of averages have always lopped off my limbs. Pretty soon, if this dry spell keeps up, I'm going to have to start patronizing online escorts…if any of them service the mountains of Southwest Virginia, which is unlikely.

He looks familiar, the fuckable one, dragging downed limbs through the pale scatter of sawdust. He looks like Bob, the sexy, scruffy way Bob used to look when he still lived in Appalachia. This realization makes my head hurt harder. I snarl another curse at the men I don't want and the cub I can't have. I spit at the windowpane, watch a few bubbles of saliva slide down the glass. Violent but harmless gestures like that make me feel good, help me believe I have a little piss and vinegar left.

In the bathroom, I pop an ibuprofen and splash cold water on my face. The man in the mirror isn't bad for fifty, got to admit. He and I rub some anti-aging lotion into our face. "I'd fuck you," I say. "Now here's one hot man left to love," I say, grinning at the glass. He grins back, of course. Shaved head, bushy gray beard. Tattoos. Solid chest and arms from weightlifting in the basement, when my slowly failing joints allow it. The booze belly found on most mature mountain men. Lots of chest hair, still black along the edges. But right between my pecs, the hair's turned white, a patch of snow slowly spreading, never melting. Each month's a blizzard adding its inches of silver, every day without requited desire's an ice storm bleaching the world to a glisten clean and simple as bone. The white birch in the backyard—February's last ice storm splintered its every bough. Weak wood. I can relate. What're weightlifting and tattoos if not attempts to harden what's congenitally sensitive and soft? You have to be pretty tough to live around here.

I pull on flannel lounge pants, socks and moccasins, a wifebeater. My nipples, after years of on-again, off-again rough play, are pretty prominent, nubbing up the ribbed white fabric. I play with them a little—they're super sensitive, they get hard fast, and my dick immediately joins them in solidarity—but I still have too much of a headache to jack off. Instead, I pull on a P-Town sweatshirt and head downstairs, followed by cats who sense the possibility of fresh food. I feed them, make a pot of coffee, light up a fire on the hearth, put on the soundtrack to *Braveheart*, and pick up *The Homeric Hymns*. The damned chain saws have stopped for the moment; I want to use the silence while it lasts.

A middle-aged, single, gay professor living in a small mountain town, addicted to the gods of literature and the heroes of cinema, his walls decorated with mounted swords. Pathetic contrast, I'm well aware, that awful gap between fantasy and reality. I can't wait to admire Gerard Butler's black beard and bare chest as the sword-swinging Spartan Leonidas in *300*—no doubt a DVD I'll be obliged eventually to own. Gerard can join the other members of my harem: Tim McGraw in his *Greatest Video Hits*, Russell Crowe in *Gladiator*, Eric Bana in *Troy*, Viggo Mortensen in *The Lord of the Rings*. Bless the technology that allows me to spend evenings with handsome, bearded men... even if I can't touch them, strip them, bind them, gag them, and ride them hard, except in Kleenex-filling fantasy.

Bearded men. Gerard, Tim, Russell, Eric, Viggo. Today's tree butcher. Bob. I've always been attracted to men with beards, but now that mine is all gray, it's the unadulterated darkness of younger men's beards that turns me on. Brown of forest animals' fur, black of storm cloud, of country nights far from office building and street lamp. Dark fur on a handsome face means youth, possibility, virility, the things I had once and have pretty much run out of.

The chain saw's resuscitated roar jolts me out of my longing and my regret. I put down *The Homeric Hymns*—beautiful black-haired Dionysos has just been kidnapped by pirates—and stand at the window, admiring the fuckable Asplundh cub's dark goatee. It's a cool, gray morning—supposed to rain later, then snow—but the effort he's putting into handling the maples' amputated limbs must have already worked up a sweat, because, to my transfixed delight, he's pulled off his down vest and opened his flannel shirt a few buttons. His chest is so black with hair there's no winter-pale flesh evident, just that midnight mat, no doubt musking up with scent. I wonder if he's ever been offered money for sex. I seriously doubt it, but still, I wonder what he'd charge. I'd pay a good bit to run my fingers and my tongue through that vigorous darkness on his chin and torso.

Bob was that hairy. Chest hair, belly hair, black goatee, receding hairline. Big pecs, beer belly, wide and sunny grin. What a beautiful bear he was. I wish I had something—a jockstrap, a pair of underwear, a T-shirt—that still retained his scent. All I have is a few photos: Bob in a mountain meadow with his shirt open, Bob sprawled by the pool at Roseland, and, best of all, Bob in our room at the Beekeeper Inn, naked, bound, and gagged on that big bed beneath the eaves.

So I own photos from many years ago. So I can stare at that beautiful, distant man sweating across the street. What good's the maddening sight of him when I'm denied his touch, his taste, his scent? I don't want to want the inaccessible Asplundh cub anymore. I don't want to hurt over those photos of Bob in my desk. *Cui bono*—What good does it do? Besides, Bob doesn't look that way any longer.

Instead, I return to "The Hymn to Dionysos." The pirates try to tie Dionysos up—a compulsion I recognize—but his godlike power frees him. The ropes fall from his hands and feet. He's not to be bound, not to be kept. His are a madness and a sweetness that come and go when they will. The wild god was in me, was in Bob. No longer. Dionysos has moved on. He and Bob left my life a long time ago.

Bob and I had a few good years. I met him at Charleston's bear and leather bar, the Tap Room, back when we both were young, still in our thirties, still living in West Virginia. There I was, my usual shy self, drinking alone in a corner of the bar, the night he won the Mountain State Bear Contest. There he was on the tiny stage, like a bare-chested god, in boots and jeans, grinning as drag queens draped the black-leather-and-silver-studs sash over his shoulder. The hairy chest, thick pecs, and beer belly had my libido, sure, but it was that black-goateed grin that snagged my heart. When I feel sadism and tenderness at the same time, I know I'm in trouble. Somehow I got the courage to buy him a bourbon after he left the stage in triumph. Amazingly, he seemed as interested in me as I was in him. My gut was smaller then, my muscles harder, my beard as black as his. He bought the second round, then, emboldened by booze, I invited him home. Pretty soon, we were groping one another in my truck on the way back to my place on Gauley Mountain, and then he was naked on my bed, playing with his own nipples, and I was uncoiling rope.

Porn producers would have had one hell of a movie if they'd managed to film our fucking that first night, or, for that matter, any of the nights after. He was the hottest man, the best bottom, I ever had. Three months later, he gave up his little apartment in Parkersburg and moved in with me. We were together for five years. I guess my heart was only strong enough to contain passion like that once, because I've never felt such ardor before or since. It's like my chest was a ceramic censer that held fire and incense for a time, then cracked with the heat and has been useless ever after. What good's a pile of potsherds? Might as well bury them, let them melt back into the earth, do some tree- or flower-roots some good.

Well, Bob left me for the city, really. Ken was only a convenient stepping-stone. As soon as Bob and I broke up, he started dating Ken. Six months later, they moved to DC.

I'd lived in DC right after graduate school, back in my twenties. Thought I'd collect a string of sexy city men, wow the world with my talent, learn how to be cosmopolitan. Hell. Teaching college English didn't make me enough money to afford to rent a Dumpster in DC, much less the handsome downtown bachelor pad I wanted. I don't know what those folks do for a living, those people living in turreted townhouses in Georgetown and Dupont Circle, but it isn't liberal arts. I endured the several-hour daily commute, the snagged traffic, the constant rush, the urban brusqueness, the comments about my accent and rusty pickup truck for exactly one year before I hightailed it back to my mountains, where folks talked like me, liked the same down-home foods, used the same Southern manners, listened to the same country music. Sure, I was queer, and I was pretty open about it, but I was also butch enough for most hill folk to accept me, if sometimes a mite grudgingly. I was queer, but I was *their* queer, if you know what I mean. If you're slender and effeminate in the country, you're fair and squarely fucked, but if you come across like just another good ole boy, albeit one who beds men, you're tolerated, especially if you're big enough to defend yourself.

So I was doing just fine living on Gauley Mountain when I met Bob. I'd had my city experience. He hadn't. It was the only spot where we might fracture. And we ever so slowly did. He was always wanting to make the long drive up to DC for three-day weekends, eager to hit art galleries, museums, restaurants and boutiques. That was all nice, two or three times a year, in my opinion, but I'd rather go camping at Dolly Sods, or hike the Cranberry Glades, or dig into heaps of fried potatoes and wild onions at Richwood's Ramp Festival, or watch beefy forestry students compete at Elkins' Forest Festival, or eat too many pancakes at Kingwood's Buckwheat Festival, or spend a few days in the isolated little hamlet of Helvetia, enjoying the quiet, wooded countryside and the hearty Swiss food. The Mountain State was enough for me.

Not for Bob. After a few years, restless, he started going to DC without me. He slept around some, guys he met at DC bars. I didn't mind that, since I had a boy named Larry who came up from Marmet sometimes to get roped and plowed. My relationship with Bob was pretty open sexually from the get-go. It wasn't other men I feared. It was the city, or, rather, what wonderful life Bob thought he was missing in the city. When he started getting the *Washington Post* and looking at job ads, the fights began. When he applied for a security clearance, I knew we were sunk. I was experienced enough to know that if you stand between a man and his longing, any love he feels for you will sour. If he'd stayed with me in West Virginia, he would've learned to hate me. If I'd moved with him to DC, I would've learned to hate him.

So that's how the great love of my life ended. The fights became silences, silences interrupted by fewer and fewer civil words. I felt like I was in a rowboat on black water at night, without oars, without any indications of where land might be. When Bob brought home a case of the crabs from his most recent fuck-fest in DC, I went into a rage. The next weekend, I went camping without him at Seneca Rocks. When I got home, he and his things were gone.

So, Ken, Bob's next husbear? Ken was a top-notch fuck, that's for sure. Redneck boy from Montgomery Bob and I had picked up at the Tap Room during our third year together. Ken had a funny little tight-assed stride, super-smooth skin, a sparse patch of chest hair, a brown beard, and a big dick. That first time with Ken was the last time I barebacked. Ken roped Bob to a chair in the corner, then cuffed my hands behind my back, tied my own wife-beater between my teeth, shoved me onto the bed, and fucked me using only spit—no condom, no lube. It hurt like hell for a while, but soon enough I was grunting with gratitude. So hot to be all roped up and helpless, getting my ass pounded while Bob watched. Nice change of pace, since with Bob I was always Top. The three of us played like that several times over a couple of years, with the addition of condoms I insisted on for future scenes. Ken really knew how to hammer a hole.

Sometimes we'd trade places: Bob on his belly on the bed, me tied to the chair. I loved how Bob's butt would rise to meet Ken's thrusts; I loved the happy, muted noises Bob would make with Ken's briefs stuffed in his mouth and Ken's cock stuffed up his ass. Afterward, Ken would spend the night, sleeping so sturdy and warm between us. Bob would make us all biscuits and gravy the morning after, or buckwheat cakes with sausage.

As butch as Bob was, as wild as his erotic appetites were, he sure knew how to keep a nice home and whip up fine meals. I used to tease him about his subscription to *Martha Stewart Living*, but secretly I was very thankful to have a man who was so good at making a cozy life for us. Soon after he moved into my unkempt Gauley Mountain farmhouse, he was buying new curtains and bath towels, planting hyacinth bulbs and unpacking his slew of cookbooks. Add his beautiful face and hairy body, his scruffy-redneck look, his always-hungry hole, and his love for ropes and gags to that sweet domestic streak, and you have the perfect husband. He was perfect for me. Except for that yearning for urban delights, something we soon realized he shared with Ken.

I guess Bob must have started meeting Ken behind my back about the time our marital fights began to slide into bitter silence. I know the sex was good between them, which is to say Ken could top Bob just as well as I could...better, I suppose, since his dick was bigger by a bit. Plus I know they both talked a lot about how much more exciting it would be to be gay in the city. I also know that Bob moved in with Ken right after he left me. Soon enough they'd found jobs in DC, had a farewell party at the Tap Room, loaded up the U-Haul, and were gone.

What I don't know is how long they were savoring the glamorous urban life they'd dreamed of before Bob began to face the fact that his new husband was fast becoming an alcoholic. Mutual friends told me all about it. Ken called in sick to work or showed up in the office hungover. He lost one job after another, spilled a martini on Bob's laptop, got slur-speeched and staggery every night. He missed the mountains, missed his family and the slow, familiar ways of West Virginia living. And so the big bear attached to that big dick that felt so good up my ass, and, no doubt, up Bob's, became, to use mountain-speak, "no account," "do-less," i.e., not worth a damn, because of his misery and drunken homesickness. The city he'd so badly hankered after wrecked him. After a year, Bob and Ken had broken up. Ken returned to West Virginia to move in with his parents and drink up his welfare checks.

Bob stayed. He loved the city, the city loved him.

All morning the tree-butchers work. By the time the predicted afternoon thunderstorm blows in, the goateed cub has unbuttoned the front of his shirt, and I'm going to the window every other Homeric page to admire his curly torso-pelt. Spring rain peppers the panes. Spring rain can touch him, though I can't. My eyes aren't sharp enough to see, but I'm sure raindrops are beading in his chest and belly hair, glistening in the pearl gray light. Soon after the rain begins, the crew calls it a day. Sexy Cub climbs into a truck, as do his buddies, and the whole pack of them drives off, leaving scattered twigs and limbs to line Seventh Street, the gray of the bark going black with wet. They'll no doubt be back tomorrow to torture what untamed trees are left.

Grateful for the silence, I put a few more logs on the fire—don't have to drive in to teach today—pour some Irish whiskey just to warm up, and, without the Asplundh cub's hairy chest to distract me, spend the rest of the afternoon finishing off *The Homeric Hymns*. By cocktail time the rain's turned cold and steady, and I'm already buzzed. I savor a few Manhattans, then heat up leftover corned beef and cabbage. It's a recipe Bob taught me. How I loved his country cooking. It kept both our bear-bellies intact. I was always pulling up his T-shirt and kissing on his hairy belly.

After dinner, nicely drunk, warm and sentimental, I put on some Celtic music, stretch out on the couch, and pull a comforter over me. Logs gutter, spit, and crumble in the grate. I close my eyes and imagine the tree-butcher cub tied to my bed, his dark eyes widening as I smooth duct tape over his mouth. I push a hand beneath my sweatshirt and run my fingers through my own chest hair. Cupping my whiskey-limp crotch, I try to remember the lovemaking Bob and I shared before things went wrong.

The Beekeeper Inn at Helvetia, empty save for ourselves. Night rain hard outside, filling up the trout stream, dripping off the spruce boughs surrounding the inn. We've had a great day, walking country roads past fields of cattle and goats, seeing signs of spring in the tiny white bells of snowdrops, the first buttery flowers of forsythia. We've sated our bear-appetites on the rich and tasty Swiss food served at the local restaurant: homemade cheeses and sausages, fried potatoes, and sauerkraut. We've gotten a good bourbon-buzz going, thanks to the flask I brought. Now I've got votive candles flickering around this high little bedroom tucked under the roof. This is our first romantic travel-weekend together, and I want it to be perfect.

Bob's standing before me, head bowed, waiting to be told what to do. He likes to obey.

"Strip," I say, and he does, pulling off his hiking boots, jeans, and WVU sweatshirt, revealing a burly body as rich with fur as the surrounding mountains are wild with woodland. "Leave the jock," I say, and he does. Bob stands there in the chill of the room, staring at the floor and shivering. He knows how hot and vulnerable I think he is wearing nothing but a jockstrap.

Bob jumps nervously when I wrap my arms around him, then sighs and hugs me hard. Gently I buckle the studded leather dog collar around his neck and lead him to the bed. Pulling back the covers, then kissing his stubbly cheek, I say, "On your belly, hands behind your back." Within minutes I've tied his wrists, roped his elbows together, and bound his ankles. It's one of God's greatest gifts, a man this strong and butch who allows me such intimacy and consents to such helplessness.

I pull off my boots and clothes now, goose-pimpling fast, and climb into bed, pulling the covers over us. Wrapping an arm around Bob, I snuggle up against him and pull his head onto my shoulder. I cup the meat of his chest in my hands, softly tousle his belly-mat. The candle flames shudder and jump. Sign of a ghost, my grandmother would have said. Outside, cold March rain drums the eaves, making music on the roof. The sound makes me solemn.

"You smell good," I say. Bob doesn't use deodorant most days just so I can savor his scent.

"Thank you, Sir." He grins up at me and rubs his goatee against my neck. He knows how much I love it when he calls me "Sir." He knows how besotted I am with him. He may be tied up, but I'm the one entirely bound.

With my free arm, I grab the flask off the bedside table, take a swig, then carefully give him a sip.

"I want to hold you and listen to the rain. In a little bit, I'm going to suck your cock till you're just this side of shooting. Would you like that?"

His "Yes, Sir" is so quiet it's almost inaudible.

Gripping his jaw, I kiss him. I kiss him for a long time, our noses rubbing, our tongues exploring, our beards brushing together.

"You want to be gagged now, I'll bet." I clamp one hand over his mouth and with the other start fondling his nipples. His torso is so hairy it takes me a second to find the smooth areolas and the hard little nubs. He shudders, nods, and grunts beneath my hand, pushing his chest against my roughening touch. I lift my hand off his face just long enough to reach for the ball-gag on the bedside table. I push the fat ball between his teeth, leaving the leather straps dangling.

"Keep it in there," I order.

Another nod, precious gesture of obedience.

"I'll buckle it in later. Later, I'm going to make these ache"—I tug on one nipple and Bob nods again—"and then I'm going to prop your butt on a pillow and eat it for about half an hour"—Bob nods, I take another flask-sip—"and then I'm going to ride you till you hurt. Would you like that?"

Another nod. I move the ball around in his mouth a little, till I can feel his saliva on my hand.

"Rope not hurting you?"

Bob shakes his head.

"Happy?"

Bob nods enthusiastically. Candle flame leaps and spits.

"Me too." I shift us onto our sides, work a nipple with one hand, and stroke his jock with the other. Soon he's breathing hard through his nose, groaning around the ball. With his bound hands, he fumbles for my cock, finds it, grips it, and nudges its head against his warm crack. Is there anything sweeter than a hairy, macho guy who loves to be bound and gagged, who lives to take it up the ass?

Later, after I've fucked Bob into a state of well-plowed rapture but before I've untied him, I'm going to take a few snapshots. I'm experienced enough to know how quickly ecstasy can decamp. I want proof, in the face of whatever losses the future might bring, that, one night at least in my life, the world was exactly the way I wanted it. Once I made love to an absolutely beautiful and desirable man, held him helpless in my arms, and my touch made us both as happy as mortal limits allow.

Bob grunts impatiently. He pushes his ass back against my crotch, pushes his chest forward against my fingers. In answer, I rub my hard-on against him and dig my fingernails into his nipple till he whimpers. I admire a man who can take a little cruelty. The candle flame leaps again, bobbing wildly, filling the room with a weird shuddering shift between shadows and light.

"Buddy boy, you are going to be sore tomorrow," I say, buckling the gag's leather straps behind his head good and tight. Rolling him onto his back, I lift his legs onto my shoulders, cup his hairy buttcheeks in my hands, and begin chewing his stiff jock, its fabric full to bursting. The gag-muffled groans he makes are as poignant and haunting a melody as tonight's chilly mountain rain.

Rain's turned to snow. I can see flurry-flakes drifting past the windows. Nothing left but broken embers, a glow and shimmer in the grate. Tonight that's all I want to remember, those times I made love to Bob. What a rough and beautiful captive he made, his hairy muscles roped up, bulging and sweating with mock-struggle. What rapturous noises he made with a gag strapped in his mouth and my cock pushed up his ass. But whiskey's insufficient amnesia. The other things, the unwelcome things, now it's their turn in memory's Möbius strip.

Before I saw his transformation face-to-face, I'd heard all about it. Not from Bob. My perfect husband turned ex, he and I lost touch right after we'd broken up. He claimed that he still wanted to be friends, but I ached for him too much to tolerate that. How could I be around him and not touch him, or watch other men touch him when I couldn't? Even his emails made me hurt. So I'd told him to fuck off, and I'd avoided the Tap Room, where, word was, he and Ken often held court, and then the happy couple, full of hopes and ambitions, had moved to the city. No, I heard about New Bob from mutual friends, Keith and Tony. They were buddies Bob and I used to drink with at Windows, the upstairs bar on Seventeenth Street where the DC bear crowd used to meet for Friday cocktails.

I refused to believe he'd changed so much. Keith and Tony swore they weren't making it up. After Ken the Drunk returned to the hills, after Bob enjoyed a few years of playing the field, he'd settled down. He had a new husband, also named Bob, a sleek, hairless little thing who could only talk about fashion, about the latest circuit party, about the newest designer drug, about his expensive home appliances, about his impressive salary, about his stock portfolio and his gym schedule. And—this is the part I couldn't take in, refused to grasp—under his new husband's tutelage my ex-love Bob had a new look. He was, in fact, someone else entirely.

Since they shared the same name, maybe that made it easier to assimilate, to merge, easier for Country Bob to become his husband, Urban Bob. I'm thinking about natural selection, adaptation. Was it something like that? The salamander species transforms in caves, becoming blind. The moth species darkens over generations, blending in with bark begrimed with industrial smoke. The chameleon turns brown against a dead leaf, green against spring grass, and disappears.

So here I go again, despite all the whiskey. I want booze to give me sufficient weight, the inertia necessary to resist. I want not to be moved, not to be dragged back by reminiscence and its damned dragline, its fucking grappling hook. Here and now is bleak—embers, snow flurries, and, yes, I'd pay that tree-butcher boy a few hundred bucks just to sleep with me, no bondage, no fucking, just his hairy, solid body heat wrapped in my arms for the night—but this cold skeleton of the present wouldn't be half so bad without the warm flesh of the past set right beside it in the same vivid field of vision.

So here we go again, and here I am again, visiting DC that last time. Long way from Gauley Mountain, from my midthirties, from the hyacinths Bob used to plant around the farmhouse my shaky finances finally forced me to give up. Why didn't anyone tell me Bob might be at the rehearsal? Since I didn't ask after him anymore, I guess everyone assumed I'd recovered. Ten years had passed. I'd changed jobs, moved to Virginia. Keith and Tony must have figured I was over the heartbreak. That would have been a safe assumption, I guess, if I had a normal heart. I'd had my share of tricks since Bob, even a few semisteady boyfriends. Anyone with any sense would have moved on, I know that.

I hate that fucking city. I've never been back.

So, DC, it's snowing a little, very windy, flurries jitterbugging down New York Avenue. Tony and I duck out of the cold and into the church. We're standing around the basement hallway, shaking snowflakes off our leather jackets, waiting for rehearsal to wind down, waiting to take Keith across the street to Café Mozart for a late dinner of hefty German food, good grub for a cold night. Keith should have been done with the Gay Men's Chorus by eight PM, but of course things are running late. As a country boy, I was brought up to be prompt, but these city queers, they're never on time, and it pisses me off. It's rude to make people wait.

I'm staying with Keith and Tony for the weekend, so I can buy some gay books at Lambda Rising, eat some good ethnic food—during my time with Bob, I developed a real taste for his German, Italian, Mexican and Thai cooking—and hit the Eagle and the Green Lantern, maybe find a cub or two who need some Tie-Time. That's about all the good a city has to offer, in my opinion: books, restaurants, and leather bars. I sample those pleasures and then get the hell out.

The honed blend of male voices reverberates in the next room. The song's "Crazy World," Tony tells me. He knows I don't care jack-shit about Broadway, but I've got to admit it's a very pretty melody. There's a lot of shouting, laughing, and commotion as the music ends, the scraping of chairs, and then the doors open and out they come, a slew of well-groomed guys. About time. It's pushing nine. I'm ready for a big stein of German beer and some sauerbraten.

Keith shouts over the noisy seethe, "Lemme get my coat," and Tony says, "Lemme hit the john," and they're off in opposite directions. Introvert from Day One, I head for a corner to escape the moving stream of strangers. Most of them are too clean shaven and slight for me to flirt with anyway. Instead I think about the meal to come. I might really indulge and have some linzer torte for dessert. Bob used to bake me linzer torte for Valentine's Day.

That's when I hear his voice, in the midst of my greedy pastry deliberation. He's calling my name.

I turn, startled, confused. I stare at the well-dressed men

passing by, milling around me. It takes me a few seconds to recognize him. The voice is the same—low, rich—but the face and body are another's. For years after our breakup, I used to dream that he would suddenly appear, out of a morning mist lit up by sunrise, out of a tulip-tree grove bright yellow with October. He would approach me like this, grab my hand, hold me close, and the sickening separation would end.

But this isn't him. The black goatee is gone. He's clean shaven. There isn't any five o'clock beard-shadow. Even his smile is different. It's guarded now, not broad and sunny. The chest hair that used to curl over his collar is gone. The unbuttoned gap at the top of his polo shirt shows smooth, shaved white skin. And the big chest, beefy arms, and bear belly are all gone. He must have lost fifty pounds since last we met. Now he has the lean waist and mildly muscled torso of an in-shape teenager.

I'm so stunned, so on automatic, Polite Pilot I like to call it, that what he says and what I say, that's all lost. I get the name of the man he's introducing me to—his husband Bob—but I already knew that. Slender guy, clean shaven, balding, handsome, aloof, in khakis and yellow dress shirt. Slip of a thing, half my size. I could break him over my knee. He's civil, but he seems less than impressed with my scuffed boots, beat-up leather jacket, graying beard, and stocky frame. Around him, suddenly I'm self-conscious about my accent, the drawn-out vowels and diphthongs that mark me as a Southern mountain man, an accent, I notice, that My Bob seems to have lost.

So you're the rough and trashy hillbilly my lover wisely dispensed with so long ago, that's what's in City Bob's eyes as we shake hands. *Ridiculous overweight hick*.

He's a corporate lawyer, I catch that much. They share a townhouse in Georgetown. They went to Paris last Christmas. I try to smile. Manners are everything. I keep looking at My Bob, trying not to stare, trying to remember who he used to be. A vague memory coalesces again and again, and again and again it dissipates, flowers of the pear trees back home, flowers falling apart on windy April days, scattering white petals all over my truck bed, as if I were hauling snow.

Bavarian wheat beer. It tastes like cloves. Ten minutes after Bob^2 have gone on their way, I'm drinking the first of what will prove to be six beers in Café Mozart. The sauerbraten comes with spaetzle and red cabbage, and it's all as delicious as Keith and Tony had promised. I have the linzer torte too, with whipped cream on the side. It's almost as good as the ones Bob used to bake.

I'm weaving a little on the walk back to the car. My friends are kind. They try to explain what's happened. They use terms I know little to nothing about: circuit boys, crystal meth, Ecstasy. They drive me back to their place, help me up the stairs. They strip me, tuck me into the guest bed.

When I shuffle down the hall and wake them in the middle of the night, when I beg them, they get out the condoms and the lube, they kiss my face and chest and cock. They ease me onto my hands and knees, and then they give it to me at both ends, a big bearded man riding my face, a big bearded man riding my ass. They fill me up as best they can. I sob and grunt, wince and slobber, rock forward onto one cock, rock backward onto another. I'll never be able to thank them enough.

I'm unsteady with bourbon to begin with, and the front walk's slippery with snow, and these cowboy boots don't have much tread. But I need to fetch it tonight, or it's liable to be hauled off by Asplundh tomorrow. I stand for a while looking up at the pale circular stubs where lopped-off branches used to be. They look like full moons, mouths agape, holes in love letters, little lakes of shaved skin. I rub my chill-stiff hands—wish I'd brought gloves—then I start collecting.

Snow dusts the street as I fill my arms. The bastards have left a good bit here. Branches, twigs—this will last me awhile, once it's dried out. Good kindling, warm fires, warm as a young man's nakedness.

Five armfuls, and the street's clean, the woodshed's a little fuller. On the back porch, I hold my hands out in the dark, let snowflakes land and melt in my palms. Inside, with a poker I break up the remaining andiron embers, then pull off my boots and drop them on the hearth. I strip to my briefs and stand by the window, watching the lawn slowly whiten.

Once, long ago, Dionysos appeared in the smoke, and the god's hair was black upon His face and upon His chest and belly, the god's body was young and strong, thick and hairy and ripe. Grapevines sprang from the black mountain earth, bears sported in the pines. The god fed me dark bread and wildflower honey, musky-sweet wines. With ivy vines, He allowed himself to be bound. The god glowed with surrender, sighed with sacrifice. Dionysos delighted my heart. He opened himself to me, the ache of earth for seed.

Shivering, I curl beneath the comforter on the couch. Spring snow is spotting the windows, assassinating the hyacinths. There's something gleaming there, on the hearth, on my boot soles. It's sawdust, I guess, wet sawdust, but in the fire's last glow it looks like sunset sweat, like powdered gold.

DRUG COLORS

Erastes

London is black and white in 1978. It's a violent hurrah—a feeling that the world is going to hell, but that's all right, because you can get there with Johnny and Sid and it won't take that long. Just three chords, blue pills and we'll all die trying.

A Bolshie freedom slides through the city with a brash overconfidence. Clubs proliferate and the straight and the not-so-straight and wish-they-weren't-straight all congregate where the queers are.

Mike passes out his Sobranies. They impress as they were meant to do. Mike buys them cheap, packetless and slightly dented, from a man in a turban down Brick Lane. They add a tawdry glamour, which would be the name of the band Mike would start if he could be arsed. He exhales, stubs out his black fag on the leather-boy on his left, and kisses the flattop blond boy on his right. The boy is pretty, his vacant eyes glow like tonic water under ultraviolet. The boy's hands fumble beneath the table; a promise for later or just a cock-tease? Hard—hard to tell. Mike demands payment. Their lipsticks stick like glue, just for a second. Mike contemplates whether he should taste him again but before he finishes the thought he's forgotten it. The table is crammed with young men, cute as puppies in baskets and desperate to be debauched so they can write home and tell their friends how wicked they are. And Mike's glad of it.

Such a few short years, Mike thinks, watching the blow-ins from Oxford and Falmouth as they shrug off the jeans of their respectability and smear themselves with the eyeliner of the city. From underground we come, and step blinking into the light, still negative, still neutral. These boys come, never ending waves of slender, Doc Martin–wearing nymphs, not for the work, but for the dole. For the music. For the cock. For the freedom. For a place that isn't the village hall on a Friday night where you'd be grateful for a fumble from anyone. For a city that swallows them all to the root, swallows them whole, then spits them out onto the Meat Rack so they can facilitate their own destruction.

The music throbs in time with the boy's grating teeth: amphetamine-fueled. Mike puts an arm around his thin shoulders and devours his mouth; there's a tang of chalk and a taste of open spaces. The puppies watch and learn, their eyes jealous, and Mike winks at one with bright white hair and a nose-ring, a copy of Mike's own. Bright-White's mouth is large and suddenly, obscenely, he sticks out his tongue and touches his shadowed chin with it. Mike decides he'll leave with him if Aston doesn't come. He likes the feel of stubble between his legs, and a long tongue can be trained in all sorts of ways.

When Aston isn't around, Mike's grateful for his age. Grateful that he still looks twenty-five in the club lights, thirty outside; grateful that Iggy Pop is no spring chicken. He affects an Iggy-skin, all battered leather, too-tight jeans and a world-weary pose that he hopes is magnetic. Grateful for his sparse frame, his abs, his South London accent, his history and his contacts—or his promise of them. They gravitate to Mike, these blow-job blow-ins, like hummingbirds losing their colors in the struggle to be noticed.

"I know a bloke at *Time Out*—could be something for you there," he says to the boy with the hand on his crotch. The gratitude shimmers in his face, and Mike takes something from the young man's mouth he'll never give back, then pushes some pills into the boy's free hand as he feels his own zip lowering. *Quid pro quo*. Sometimes it's the possibility of a job at Rough Trade, a casting call with Jarman, the chance of gophering at the Palais. It doesn't matter. The boy smiles prettily, says something over the music, but whatever he says doesn't matter and is lost in the beat, anyway. Mike pushes the pretty smile down into his lap.

There's a wave of excitement from the litter of boys and Mike tenses. He stops his studied pose when Aston walks in. For all the frenetic thrusting of the place, the up and down of the dancers, the rhythm of the mouth on his cock, everything seems to still when Aston, real name Martin—a joke that has gone beyond cliché and has entered into legend—pulls respect to himself as easily as he does the hyena-eyes of the new boys. Then they cluck like chickens, the floor show of Mike forgotten.

"He's slept with Jordan..."

"He's fucked Adam..."

"He's forming a band..."

"His cock is pierced..."

"I'm going to try..."

Mike doesn't need to hear the gossip; he knows it all—started a lot of it. He waits, waits in the dark, more excited by Aston's prowl toward the bar than he is with the boy who is now kneeling under the table. He leans back again, his heart thudding in his chest, and waits for Aston to stop fucking around, which he does, eventually, turning toward the darkened booth with a heart-stopping smile. He towers over them all, looking like Goliath in his platform motorcycle boots, his tartan kilt, his impossibly high hair.

The band stops, and the lead singer starts spouting poetry as bad as anything Mike has ever heard. Aston sits; the chains around his legs clackity-clack against the metal chairs. He fixes Mike with a stare, pupils as huge as the moon, and pouts.

"New?"

Mike wonders how he does this, how he always manages to make his entrance when there's space and quiet enough to speak. Does he wait outside? Does he bribe someone? He's never seen him do it, although he's wealthy enough, Daddy's shame in tartan and tattoos. Drummed out, all the way from Pimlico.

"Mostly," Mike answers. The boy on the floor has given up; he's flat on the sticky carpet, his mouth open, staring up at the remnant glitterball high in the club ceiling. Mike zips himself up with a smirk. He can't remember the litter's names so he doesn't bother with them. Aston wouldn't care who they were, and they know it, they cast around for lesser prey.

"Seen George?"

"Yesterday," Aston says. "Sends his love. I thought I'd bring it." He spouts bullshit about his absence, been filming, he says.

Mike listens and tries not to show how pleased he is to see him. He knows Aston's lying; he knows Aston went home for the monthly lecture and payout. He doesn't care. He stands up and takes Aston's hand. "Come on," he says. "I'm not staying here." He grabs his beer, takes the blow-job boy's beer for Aston, and they split.

They stagger out onto the narrow pavement and take control of the night. Tourists stop and stare; they point at the madness of Aston's hair and when they try and take pictures Aston gets aggressive, ends up kicking a waste bin over, the papers spilling out to join the crap already littering the streets. They jump the barrier at Oxford Circus, and run down the escalator laughing like drains.

All the way home they play for the train. They behave like they are expected to. Aston spits on the floor, Mike swears like he's got Tourette's. They sing "Hurry up Harry," their boots crashing in time against the slatted wooden floors, and make obscene gestures the way they've seen Rotten do. They glower at the travelers from under kohl-rimmed lashes. When they kiss, Aston devours Mike's face like some kind of maniac and a man and his wife get up and move into the next carriage. Aston gives him the finger, and gropes Mike's crotch, just for fun. "It's fucking legal!" shouts Aston. He stands and swings around on the pole. He yells over and over again. "It's fucking *legal*! Live with it!"

Mike's reminded of a wildlife program, the stags bellowing in rut, and he giggles uncontrollably, falling against the woman next to him, who moves away. "You're my stag, man. You're my stag."

Back in Mike's squat they share a line before fucking—broken mirror, McDonald's straw. They hardly undress, first time. Boots and bondage too hard to cope with in the speed of the lust.

Aston takes control, all jealous need. He pushes Mike over the back of the settee. His trousers hit the floor with a clank. "Baby-bird suck you off?" he says as he pulls Mike's cock out with a possessive air.

"Couldn't manage it."

"Gettin' old, old man."

"Was thinking of you." He gasps as Aston pushes in, straightens up so he's closer. "They like it. You like it."

"I do," Aston says. "Would have watched if he hadn't passed out. What's in those pills you give them?"

"Who gives a fuck?"

The coke takes the edge off, strings them out, and slowly everything focuses into details. Mike can feel every muscle in Aston's palm as it slides up and down his cock, almost too gently. Aston's hair is hard against the side of his face, his face harsh with stubble. Mike can nearly count every hair, tries to, fails.

"Fuck this," Aston says, pulling away. "Why should I do all the work?" They undress. It takes time.

Mike falls back on the bed, grabs a spike of Aston's hair and pulls him down. Aston's body is a pale wonder, slender and long, his cock the same with a subtle curve Mike knows Aston hates. Aston had wanted to dye his pubes the same pillar-box red as his head and they'd tried it, once, but Aston had ended up screaming in pain, and he'd punched Mike in the head as he rinsed off the dye, almost helpless with laughter.

When Aston tries to turn him over, he shakes his head, shuffles forward so his arse hangs off the bed. He wants to watch as Aston comes.

They'd laugh, he thinks, if they could see us now. Almost tender, almost lovers. Aston pushes back in, his eyes screwed shut, and like always, Mike wonders who he sees. It's hard not to wonder if he sees someone younger, more Adam than Iggy. He's too aware that Aston could—does—have anyone, and that he's a good fifteen years younger. That Aston shapes the world around him, and Mike is only wearing camouflage. He's scared that one day Aston will scratch the surface and find the remnants of the Isle of Wight Festival, flowers in Mike's hair, broken tambourine.

Aston is everything Mike wants, and he keeps him only by not caring. He keeps taking what the boys give him because it keeps Aston coming back, knowing he could stop Mike dead, lead him by the nose-ring, lead him to Hell and that's how they both like it.

The world turns.

They all turn around to a new beat, free of cardigans and the home counties; they steal straws from McDonald's and stock up on blues, three for a quid and no questions. The world slows in a London night, stealing time from the dancers. Lyceum and the Marquee, all blurred guilt and pogo frenzy. Adam teaches them to wear khaki, Jordan has them in bondage, and the *flick flick flick* of the tube strobe shows Aston's face, thin white duke painted white in the neon, black mouth, black nails, a lad a little insane. They fuck all night on pills and lager and Aston sits for hours in front of the mirror, saying how the black holes in his eyes will kill him—there's a hole waiting to suck him in, he says. Mike listens endlessly to Kraftwerk and feels Aston deep in his throat and heart, swollen like blood.

"One day," Aston says, "we'll fuck right off." He lights a joint and flings himself across Mike's body. Mike can't help but stroke the brittle hair, now limp and sticky around Aston's shoulders. "We'll go to Bali and drown some hippies. We'll go to New York and break the scene. Dad will pay just to see the back of me."

Mike closes his eyes as Aston sucks him in again. He feels his soul spiraling down Aston's throat. He can see the palm trees but to him they line Oxford Street and they drop blue fruit onto the crowded pavement beach.

OTHER RESIDENCES, OTHER NEIGHBORHOODS

Douglas A. Martin

1

I put my number inside *The Golden Spur*, the book he was buying, along with his receipt, hoping he'd call me. There were real bookstores in the city, ones that didn't fill their shelves with toys and candy, games and puzzles, ones not necessarily fun for the whole family. I was working in one of them. I'd picked him out, when he walked in. The boss didn't want us reading while on the clock, and so I'd watch the boys like him and men when they'd come in, waiting for someone to respond. I was hoping he'd come back to look for me. You could tell by the way that some of them looked, the way some of them would look at me, that we were alike.

Nobody met anyone's eyes where I was from originally, like everyone was afraid of everyone else, wanting what the other might not want. All shades over the windows kept pulled down, curtains kept closed, that's how they lived there. No one who had any idea of what it was like would wonder what had brought me here. There weren't a whole lot of options, and if any man had kissed me in his car, had taken a chance, putting his hand on my knee, asked me in; if any guy had showed me how he wanted me in that way, I would try my hardest to hold on to him.

He'll come back to the bookstore, in Brooklyn, Park Slope, and I'll watch him lock up his bike outside. Here you could go out for drinks and then home to his place, go to bed together, that very night. Something like love, that could make you stay anywhere.

Mostly, we'd go to his place, not mine.

Like me, he'd come from down South.

He'd be the third from that first year in the city, after the first boy who thought I liked sex too much, also not from the city; and the next, who'd like it when I came over to his place in Brooklyn Heights, sweaty, after having run around all day, already having been with somebody else, who liked it, he said, when I smelled all gamey. That's what he called it. This new one, some nights he'll fall asleep with just me stroking his hair.

One twin bed barely fit into the small room that was mine, on the top floor of a building converted into as many rentable spaces as possible, right across the street from the Wyckoff Projects, above the noisy, twenty-four-hour deli. I wasn't going to let myself grow up to be like them, men I'd known back home, the streets all crowded with their cars, though there was little else there.

It's just men who were connected through their talk of women, women's bodies, sports, yard work; close to each other only if they'd gone to the same high school; happy, content, or trying to be, with the boat for the lake, freezers full of deer meat, new cars, and houses or trailers to one day own.

We won't live in Chelsea, but we go there sometimes to housesit for one of his friends. The boy from the bookstore, it seems, likes making love in other people's beds, more than when we are just at his or my place.

We'll be up in a loft, early in the morning, trying not to make much noise, to be as quiet as possible; this turns him on, while his two friends sleep downstairs. Or we'll be in another bed in an apartment in Clinton Hill, trying to make sure, consciously, or unconsciously, that when we come, finally, we come on each other's stomachs, pressing against each other as tightly, as flat as possible, not coming all over whoever's bed.

He's friends with a librarian, whose sad, neurotic cat we tend to, who can't really be left alone, can't stand it. Thirteen, we are told he is, that's an old man for a cat. He needs more care than that.

When he retires, the friend, the librarian, he moves from one place in Chelsea to another bigger, better place. It's a move up in the neighborhood. Prime real estate. He tells us they call it the "Faggot Fortress," some of the other residents, his neighbors. It's a building that extends for blocks, that takes up a whole couple of avenues in the city, that's how expansive it is. Behind a set of doors in the new place, the bed folds down from the wall. It's called a Murphy bed.

In that same building in Chelsea, others like us will live. Others like us will love. Others like us will hold each other, move deeper inside each other, and deeper, deeper into each other, far into the night. Others are together, and one turns to the other, turns him onto his back, or the other turns onto his back, the other gets on top, or the other one turns onto his stomach, and the other one gets on top. Or maybe they stay side by side.

Some years later, another librarian, a big-deal one, one I know after the other has left town, great place or no great place in the F. Fortress he sold it, is getting everyone drunk, and we are talking not only of books. We are, after all, gay men. Here, have another glass of wine. On to porn. Here, there's some more. Another bottle.

He points at me and says he just knows how I like to take it. He's drunk.

It's not a charge. It's not like I need to defend myself.

Did he ask to know, really, what I was? Really?

I don't tell him about what I loved most, when the boy I'd be with in other people's beds would let me get on his back, would just lie down on his stomach for me. Or I don't tell him how he liked it when I'd straddle him, get on top of him, locking my legs tightly, closely, clamped onto the sides of his lower trunk, while we'd move.

That didn't mean I didn't want him to fuck me, which once upon a time I could have left or taken. Are you two anal, we'd be asked, me and the one other boy like me I'm sleeping with toward my end of high school, even in our small town. One of the couples we met in the mall, one of the two we knew, in the city of Macon, thirty minutes north, they wanted to know. If you hung around long enough, you might meet others like you, in the mall.

They'd love to hear all about it, though we weren't really doing it yet. Things moved slower there where I was from, than where I'd eventually come.

Off at college, no more waiting for parents to fall asleep, or trying to find somewhere to go during the day, to see what you could get away with, though off at college, you'd still not completely fled the nest. Another boyfriend, an older man. There was only one thing we hadn't done yet.

There were more, but I knew what he meant. It was an easy guess.

We'd take turns with each other.

Come on, he'd say, you're fucking me. And then I'd have to try to do it harder, slam into him, and he'd end up wincing, hurt, seizing up, staring at me, catching his breath, and we'd stop.

Other boys come here from somewhere else, too, who haven't grown up with and in New York City, either. Boys like me who might go from place to place, before it's all over, before they settle down, if they ever do. Boys who see how they might never have a home, if it isn't in the bed or arms of another boy.

We are driving to Buffalo. Now that we live in the city, we like to get out of it, too, me and the boyfriend from the bookstore. We are driving with new friends. One of the men is one of those theorizers of men and boys like us. We meet people like this because my boyfriend and I both want to be writers. The older, more established writer keeps saying, while my boyfriend drives, things like, he could only imagine what the two of us got up to, what we must do together.

He says my boyfriend is like the Marquis de Sade.

He's so turned on by what this man is saying, must be, about what he thinks about him, how he must be sexually, that that night in the hotel, he's going to be more wild with me than he's ever been before, after all this attention that's been paid to him, and me, all throughout the drive. Or he's just so happy to be there with me, once the man has left our room for his own.

When we two were still sleeping together, sometimes we'd run into someone one or the other of us knew. Like, when waiting for the subway together, the upstairs neighbor of my first boyfriend in New York, who asked us if we were brothers.

They show real films at the Brooklyn Academy of Music, like in Chicago, where I make sure to go see the Wakefield Poole retrospective, someone doing what he did long before I was even born, and *Hustler White*, when I'm there, thinking I might try to move there. In *Goodbye, Dragon Inn*, one man looks for another man in the theater, while the movie plays, over and over.

As a boy, I'd wanted to be in movies, because in some you could see how people lived, and felt, differently. In Chelsea, there was the Chelsea Hotel, but it was too expensive to stay there now, even just for a night, forget about someone like me trying to live there. He'd tell me how I reminded him of the boy in *The Chelsea Girls*, in one of the scenes where the film captures strips and stripes of lurid colors, as they cross the boy's face, as he is talking. First red, then green. First stop, then go. One who talks about perception, touch, apples, on his lips; salt, on his skin.

Sweet of him to say, though we both know we're aging, and he no longer will want me that way he used to, when we'd first kissed on his floor by his stereo, and he told me I didn't have to go home that night. What I remember so much feeling was the rub against the texture of his jeans.

Boys, men here, we went as far with each other as we could see ourselves, and then we moved on to the next promising prospect. Some of us still thought of ourselves as boys, not men, or guys, not fathers, not dads, and for as long as we possibly could, we would.

The day before Christmas, in Fort Greene, a boy around my age would run his hand through my hair, while I gave him head. We started with me, ended up on him, the *Lord of the Rings* DVD he had been watching paused on the TV. It felt good to be rubbed like that and there. I used to always keep it so combed, something in it. Getting all dolled up, that's what my stepfather used to say about me, when I'd be standing in front of the mirror in my bedroom or the bathroom.

After we'd both made each other come, he asked if I was doing anything for the holidays, and when I answered, asked him if he was, he said sure not going home.

2

In Brooklyn, Fort Greene, I would be living alone. No more sharing a bed in Manhattan, after she said I didn't have to sleep on the couch if I didn't want to, with a girl I'd gone to the same college as, now in the city trying to make her name as a photographer. No more sleeping in the living room, on the couch that was a futon, across from the projects, in Boreum Hill, before the area has begun being identified more easily by its one gentrifying street, Smith, where the boutiques all move in. Even that neighborhood is not safe. No more Bay Ridge, where I bring whoever I can get ahold of late at night into the living room, onto another couch that also folds out into a bed, nights I can tell how my roommate won't be returning for the evening, and when I need to feel there might be other bodies needing like I do. Try to make sure we come on the floor and not the couch.

I need to wear clothes that show I don't care too much about my appearance, and then I might appeal to the broadest possible range of tastes. If I keep my nails painted punk, that'll scare some men off. I get more outside the more I seem to blend in with the men, to on the surface be just like them, still out, late at night, the more the clearest message is the one that moves between our meeting eyes.

Granted, there may not be grounds for a relationship here.

So where was I from?

Georgia.

But that's all I'd tell some.

To the city, that's where the men who didn't want to get trapped went, if what they needed was a change of scenery, when they saw the small towns beginning to isolate them. What begins to matter more than anything are the ways we could and did come together. There were places to go, if you wanted to meet guys like you, all over the city. Some worked hard during the days, and during the nights, when others were shutting their eyes, theirs would still be open, and looking, out on the streets, in the stores, in the bars, designated in one way or another as for our kind.

I've mostly stopped lying about my name, or what I do. I'm a student, I tell them. I write. The tattoo on my wrist, I can't take it away, and it shows itself off, if I raise my arm up above my head, if I've gone inside with someone, undressed, if I've leaned back for them, gotten on my back, at least take off my shirt, really relax, do what some of them want me to do, the way they want me to. Then some ask if that's my girlfriend's name, and I have to laugh. A writer, a dead poet.

I couldn't really live in the heart of anything, not the way I was struggling, financially. I didn't sleep with Chelsea boys, I slept with Brooklyn men. I'd walk up and down, along, around the promenade late at night, out by the highway, where some of the better off in Brooklyn lived. There was an area up around there, up in Brooklyn Heights, where sometimes the men would stop their cars, open their doors, have you go with them to drive around some, until they could find somewhere dark enough to park, or they'd just begin while driving, down in the shadows of the car, steering, where they could get to your fly, get it open, get you out, look at you, hold and move it around with their one hand not on the wheel, stashing you back, dropping it, or moving you up under your untucked shirt, and putting the other hand back up on the wheel again, if at one bright corner they had to stop, behind or for other cars. Or that one right there was a police one. It could be hard to see inside them. All you had to go by, when considering whether or not you might want this or that one to slow down, try to provoke him somehow, was the kind of car he had.

They either stopped for you or they didn't. If it was just a numbers game, the more like you there were around to catch, the better luck. You caught more flies with honey, I'd been told once, when coming off so angry at the world. You'd better get this all out of your system, while you were still young. Out on the streets of the city, you had to be able to take me for what I was, what I wanted to become, I kept telling myself.

If the sorts of men you were after didn't really want to be caught, it could make for arrangements where of prime importance was only whether or not you were in the same neighborhood. Some required little else.

I'd move through different neighborhoods, like moving through different sets, tracking myself through different hands, putting myself into them, seeing who brought what out of me, how far I'd go with each, just how far I'd want to.

Depending on the boy or man, it fluctuated.

Red Hook, they called it, out toward the end of the island, where I was living underground, really, in the basement of a shacklike house, rigged for living, some electrical outlets put in, a hotplate, a space made for a shower. The ceilings were low and silver, and the whole basement felt at times like a tugboat. The moisture was kept pulled out of the air down there by a machine plugged in.

Nobody ever came inside, though I invited one or two in, kissed one boy outside the door, while he straddled and held up the frame of his bike. He'd ridden down from Cobble Hill. He laughed, because, he said, when he pulled away from kissing, he could feel my "boner," pressing against him. Then we kissed some more, and he said I was a good one.

I liked to. I didn't get to, not much. When he wanted to know how come, said I was so cute, I said something about my last boyfriend. He didn't really like to, or he'd stopped wanting to. Said something then about just having stupid men's room sex since then, for the last year or so. He himself was only kissing me because his current boyfriend never wanted to sleep with him anymore.

You lived in these compromised places, or with roommates, if you had no one in your life to share bills with you. Why didn't I just get another job? I was trying to make ends meet, and I was trying some nights not to be so lonely. I would be looking to pull myself outside of myself, for ways to get further outside me and my own tendencies.

You could be so close, and still so far. Down Coffee Street, down six or so blocks, there was the water, and out across it, the view of the Statue of Liberty. You could see some big boats going by, if you got lucky, pulling their whistles.

Another boy on a bike rides suggestively around, down by this pier in Brooklyn. Different boy, different bike. Different borough, different pier. He raises up, then lets himself back down, the seat grinding up into his body, the split between his legs, as he comes back up and then down again.

When it's obvious there's little to say, more to do, he can take me back to his place. He has a roommate, but he's probably not at home. Not at this time of the afternoon. If he's there, he can sneak me in, then back out.

When walking around there late at night, two o'clock and three in the morning, sometimes four or five, but by then the light in the sky is coming up, there are wild cats. Even in the winter, in the snow, still some.

I've taken myself to riding a bike around, a trick one, BMX, but it is old, a used one, with its mirrored silver frame, tires once detailed with gold rims, that paint now rubbed down. The chain will slip, if I ride too fast, though I mostly only use it at night, not for any real transportation, to get from one point to another, more just to slowly breeze through streets empty and deserted, especially for New York. Remarkably, for the city.

There are trucks, too, hauling things. They pull through there, or they park along one of the back streets, closer to the water, idling over there, for some later hours of the night.

Once I work myself up to riding slowly over to one, after circling around, getting brave enough to finally sidle up to the door. A short exchange, pleasant but gruff enough, culminates with the driver rubbing his crotch, like I am mine against the bike frame and my own hand, a gesture that could be brushed aside if need be. We're both horny, and he asks me if I know anywhere he could go to bang some bitches.

In Bay Ridge, Spectrum has been there forever, but it closes shortly after I move into that neighborhood. Some of the men out there don't need the bars for what they want. Some will open their doors to you, around two, late at night, around three, have a curtain already hung up and in place, which you're not to walk behind. Just stand there, in front of the curtain, and he'll reach around.

He calls it a glory hole, even though there's no wall, no hole, just his head under, around, the curtain.

The iron gate that leads to his space under the stairs is unlocked. He'll wait there for you. All you have to do is drop your pants.

Around come his hands, helping you get them open and down, coming around then again with the little brown bottle he's already taken up to his own nose hidden, offering you some now.

That's all right, you don't need it.

Oom-who, oom-who, mouth full of you, he mumbles for you to keep going, not to stop.

I'm blond, blue, roughly one hundred fifty, not smooth. Cut. Thirty-three. Appearances can be a trap. I have this, this one part of me. Top, if I fuck. With strangers. But I'm open to other things. Pretty versatile, otherwise.

Generally prefer scruffy types, I sometimes type when leaving an ad, looking to get out of the house some cheap way.

I like some of the clips on his DVD, called something like *A Hundred and One Shots*. Or *A Thousand*, like *A Thousand and One Nights*. Who could ever count so many? This man, whose house I go over to in Bay Ridge, has it going when I get there. It's all fragmented 'cause it's just for the good parts.

He wants me to find the door unlocked, when I get inside,

take off all my clothes, and see him already on the couch.

Naked and stroking, he says, wanting to know if this sounds hot to me.

Before he'll let me just come over, he wants to talk on the phone first.

I'd asked my writing teacher where he met his boyfriend, when he introduced me to him, and he said where everyone met these days, online.

In most of the "shots," the scenes setting them up, even if they've begun with only themselves, the men eventually will have someone stumble upon them, to come join them, play with them, play along. I like best ones I imagine are from the '70s, men from what appears to be this other time, dated with their mustaches, their bodies not shaved, not so all neatly groomed; muscles, bulk, or youth, thinness, not of such a seemingly set priority; in a more indeterminate state, in different ways nondescript, looking how I might like to when doing it, like a bit more than simply acting, a bit more desperate, and accepting, more accommodating, even, than purely pleasing, not so poised, at least not to my eye, trained on the here-and-now. Some things you only share with those you know are in some ways just as wanting as you. It wasn't in front of a gold-rimmed mirror anymore I was trying to convince myself I was there.

What do I want, they ask, what could they do for me, they want to know. If there was ever anything he could do for me, just let him know, one who calls me "stud" says, who asks if I like to role-play and just for a minute, once, goes into another set of words, to play with me like we're just two boys home alone. Another: You blonds, you always look so young. "Pretty boy," my stepfather had taunted. The more different I could look back then from all those rednecks, the better. There was one bar for boys like me, called the Pegasus. The boy like me and I would go around looking for more like us. I'd say stop the car, there in that stretch of the park, in Macon, where a street pulls through. That one perched there, smoking a cigarette, on the hood of his car, parked off to the side, looked like someone I might like. Looked "bohemian," an odd word at the time I liked the sound of in my mouth.

The more voices I gathered in my head, the better. The more they might build to a finer opinion, counteract, balance each other. More options. More possibilities. More ways to see myself, see how men could be and want. Then the more chances to escape.

It'll begin to tickle them, scratch at them, when I haven't shaved in a while, and I'm letting my beard grow in. In his DVD, when the scenes shift more toward what I'd guess are the '80s, the settings move to nicer ones, bigger beds, richer sheets, bigger and smoother men on them. Afterward, after we've gone through a number of the scenes, manipulating ourselves and each other, together, or I let him do to me whatever he wants, don't really object, he tells me I can sit down, relax. I don't have to put my shoes and clothes right back on just yet. I can sit on the chair with the towel he's spread out on it for me, catch my breath. Do I want a beer or something? Some offer. Some before, some after. And if I take off too immediately, some are not going to ask me back.

Let him talk to me some more about my body, while he spreads out on the couch, keeps himself nice and hard, still slick, slippery. Squeezes out a bit more lube. I used to like to get it in my mouth. We were in love, so I could take in more of him. We were only doing it to each other.

All sorts of things are said in the heat of the moment, in the throes, but he wants to talk, too. About his job. He has birds in cages and cactus in terrariums. He's a landscaper. His ex, they both still live in this building, since they broke up. His ex got to keep the front apartment, while he moved into the back of the building. But they're still on the same floor, still close. They both like the neighborhood. Still like each other.

What's wrong with me, he keeps asking. I'd seemed so removed, so distant, earlier. He asks me if I just broke up with someone. You know how it is, he says, when you're fucking around, and you're saying to yourself, what am I doing here?

His ex is a man of fewer words, almost fewer even than me. I know because some nights I go to see him, too.

Just because they're no longer interested in each other, that doesn't mean they're no longer interested in sex. He does keep saying how some night he was going to let me fuck him, wanting to know would I like that, did I want that, like that might keep me interested, coming back. But he was going to have to be ready for it. I haven't lost my restraint with him, or he with me, like slipping inside the boy between neighborhoods, on the outskirts of my old one, not just his mouth, when he pulls me back, on top of him, on his back, strong legs up around me, spurring me.

His ex wants me to enter their building quietly, to walk down the hall quietly, will emphasize mostly the way I should come and leave, makes sure I know how not to get lost in that building. When I get to the top of the staircase, go up one flight to the second floor, take a left, go down to the end of the hall. One scene in the movie he has on a couple of times when I arrive starts by showing a "soldier" alone in his military jeep, and then when he's caught with his khakis down, playing with himself over and through the steering wheel, he says something to the effect of, what would you do with one this big, Sergeant?

I was from "The International City," a joke, basically. They called it that because of everyone in the military who moved there. I used to think older men might help lead the way, might point me out of there. Sheltered, I knew, I needed to get away. Then I began to go to them because I thought I knew what I could expect from them. Believed I knew what they wanted from me.

Could he offer me a drink?

Back in Macon, this one with his life, dog, obviously expensive things, side table for his cocktails.

Something sweet.

He'll put it in some Coke.

In my class in the city, we were reading *The Ravishing of Lol Stein*. ("She says that in school—and she wasn't the only person to think so—there was already something lacking in Lol, something which kept her from being, in Tatiana's words, 'there.'") I was taking out loans from the government, ostensibly for school, and I'd defer until I couldn't any longer, I figured. Who cares if you die in debt?

In a small town, you needed to move, so you didn't keep coming across whomever, when it hadn't worked out. When I walked out of the building in Bay Ridge, I walked along a sidewalk that ran along road on one side, park on the other, a highway on the other side of the park.

A year and a half since I'd known where I could try to go at night when I just didn't want to go home, that long since I'd been with someone I didn't feel I had to protect myself from in subtle ways in sex. Then two years, three even, when I'm doing what you could call just fucking around. Or you could call it trying to see if the only thing I'd lost was a release. The city was full of alternatives.

I'd read the words wrong, sometimes in class, or mispronounce, like slips of tongue, though not quite, exactly. Things like reading "unwordly" in place of "unworldly." Maybe not a pointless juxtaposition.

Make it feel good, make it feel good for yourself, he kept saying to me, when he wanted me to control the way, the speed at which, I was going in and out of his opening.

JUNIPER HOUSE

Alana Noel Voth

for TJL

When I started my job at Juniper House everyone was happy, my parents, all the weirdos at AA, as if going to work every day should provide a person with this incredible happiness.

Juniper House was an institution for autistic kids. I cleaned rooms. The kids at Juniper would blow anyone's mind with their messes. They liked to disassemble stuff and often pulled their beds apart: blankets, sheets, and then the mattress. One kid dug a hole through his box spring, deep enough to accommodate his arm, and then stuffed food inside so it became a weird minefield of springs, stuffing and pancakes. Other kids arranged the furniture in their rooms into straight lines. The bathroom was another story. Lots of kids missed the toilet entirely, and one boy, Devon, created a display on the wall with his own shit I'd call nothing less than artistic. I stood there flabbergasted, not by the smell but by what I saw: a defined, sophisticated face. I hated cleaning it up, like I was ruining it or something, this tiny gorgeous underappreciated flex of genius.

The landscape around Juniper House was like an oasis on the edge of downtown: maple trees, wildflowers, and grass. In some ways, the landscape made me think of home. The building itself was masonry, just a building. Once in a while, I took one of the kids for a walk outside. Louie, a redhead, counted backward from one million. Lily with the shining black hair spoke Russian to daisies. Then there was Robbie, who quizzed me on math equations but never waited for my answers. Anyway, I didn't know the square root of five hundred-and-eighty-five.

The kids at Juniper weren't "high functioning," so they couldn't be allowed in school with other people's normal kids or even in the general public. Some had disappointed their families: I knew because some of them never had visitors. When I was in rehab, I didn't want visitors. When Mom showed up, I refused to see her. I wasn't sure whether these kids minded not having visitors. Once I overheard a nurse tell another nurse: "Parents need time to mourn the loss of the child they didn't have." Then I heard Mom in my head all over again crying as she came down a row of jail cells to bail me out.

One kid, Bruce, hadn't had a visitor the whole time I'd worked at Juniper House. Last Tuesday, I was in Bruce's room to clean it. I made the bed, then emptied the trash, which was when I noticed a suspicious but silky nest of hair tucked in with the snotty tissues. Was Bruce pulling hair out of his own head? Should I report this to the nurse's station? From a few feet away, I couldn't see any bald spots on Bruce's head and so decided to keep his secret. In the bathroom, I started on the toilet. That's when I heard him say, "Hi."

I stepped from the bathroom. The TV was on. Bruce sat on

his newly made bed staring at the flickering screen. "Hey Bruce. You watching MTV?"

I looked at the screen. 50 Cent or somebody rapped at a barely audible volume surrounded by a bunch of slutty looking girls. I looked at Bruce again, and for a second, he squinted his eyes at me, and I actually expected him to answer. Then he dropped his eyes and began separating marbles from a pile on his bed. "Hi. Hi. Hi."

Bruce was fifteen and looked like a young Rob Lowe. He was never going to get laid. I didn't know if that mattered to him or not. We'd only had one-way conversations.

"I haven't had cock in two months, Bruce, and it's killing me. When you're a small-town hick in the big city who can't keep a job, you don't appeal to a lot of people." The boy didn't look up. "Last time I got any action was a blow job from a guy I met in AA who invited me to a dry party, which means there wasn't any alcohol there, and seeing as I'm not drinking right now but kind of wanted to get out and stuff, I went to the party with this guy Eugene."

Bruce continued to separate marbles from the pile.

"Yeah, it's a boring story." I went back to the toilet and got a nose full of ammonia.

A minute later, Bruce appeared in the bathroom. "Do you like pie?"

"What?" I looked at him. This guy could keep me guessing, that was for sure.

Bruce leaned back and forth on his feet and smiled at me; well, not at me exactly, maybe toward me. Then Bruce turned to a mirror and gazed at himself as he swayed back and forth, and I thought, *Wonder if he understands how gorgeous he is? Except, what good would that do him since he has no interest in people or any desire to please them?*

"I envy you, man."

"I like pie," Bruce said.

I scrubbed his toilet until it shone like a pearl you'd find in an oyster.

The guy I mentioned, Eugene: he might have weighed a hundred-thirty pounds, and he had these big ears he'd pierced four times down each side, which only brought attention to how big his ears were, and he also had acne; more like cysts on his neck and chin. Other than that, he was probably attractive. Night of the party, he'd gelled his hair, gone all out. Everyone there was a recovering alcoholic, and that was all they talked about. Recovery. Dragging a cart of sins behind them. Wanting to feel normal. Eugene started to talk in my ear about a GLBT support group.

"Would you be interested in doing a newsletter?" he asked.

"What newsletter?"

"For the GLBT group."

"Why would you ask me?"

"You write."

"Who told you that?"

"Jeremy Johnson."

"Who's that?"

"Member of the GLBT support group."

"I've no idea who that is."

"He said you could write."

"I've no idea why he'd say that."

We stood there several minutes, during which time it struck me how sober I was, because I was uncomfortable, and a lame silence hung between Eugene and me while I debated admitting I did, actually, write a little but probably not well enough for a newsletter. Besides a support group meant getting socially active, hoping against hope to get involved in life, and there was this other guy at the party I found extremely cute but who was a million miles away, like out of my reach, my league; and in the middle of the last AA meeting this same guy had stood up from his seat looking glorious and golden and said: "I'm going to be that guy, you know, the one on the other side of the window we've all looked in on before, whose life is healthy and normal, you know, cut and dried, and I'm going to be *that happy*." Then he gave everyone this big glowing smile, which was hokey enough I could have vomited, but he was extremely cute, which led me to realize that night at the party that I was turned on, like my cock had moved, and the longer I looked at this cute guy whose life would become cut and dried, and therefore happy, the more I became convinced he looked like Leonardo DiCaprio. Incredible!

Pretty soon, Eugene and I were alone in a dark room. I had a serious boner and reached into the dark in front of me, around me, until I made contact with a solid mass, Eugene's chest. I felt under his shirt for his nipples. Already I was pretending he was Leonardo DiCaprio huffing cola breath in my face and trying to kiss me. Yeah, Leonardo DiCaprio interested in me, turned on by me. I grabbed his head and kissed him. My nose tickled from the smell of all the gel in his hair. Leo was an enthusiastic kisser. A vacuum. As he sucked my tongue he went for my fly, then latched on to my cock with a sweaty palm and rubber fingers before he got on his knees and worked me into his mouth. You would have thought he was stuffing a sub sandwich in there. Holy shit! Leo slobbered all over my cock, which made me remember how much I liked blow jobs. And when I came, I groaned so hard I didn't recognize the sound of myself.

I grew up in a wooded area that smelled like pasture and tree bark and animals. Ripe, sweet, a little pungent. Mom and Dad had a farmhouse. I went to a small school. Small-town boy, country, gay, and seriously bent on getting away to the big city because I'd believed in the visions of glamourous living running amuck in my head. I arrived with nothing but a backpack and a head full of urgency: *Let's live!*

Soon enough, I was crowded by masses of possibility, more like expectation, and then just a ton of failure. I lost my first job because, as the boss had put it, I was too slow, and he'd said it like I was retarded. Then I lost my second job too. And ended up in a bar. When I came out, weaving a little, blinking, the city smelled like cold dead sex. The smell had something to do with leaves pinned motionless to sidewalks by rain two hundred and fifty days out of the year. And the way everyone walked past me, right over me really, was like I was down there on the sidewalk with those poor damned leaves.

Once I created a MySpace account out of boredom and because I wanted to meet a guy in theory. I posted a picture of an actor nobody had heard of at the time but who was cute, and then I wrote a profile. *Small-town boy longs for the experience of a hot, interesting, city guy. In huge need of survival tips.* Then I got drunk for three months and forgot to check my new MySpace account. When I did, I had seventy-five new "friends." So many city guys offering to help me survive. But I chickened out; didn't believe it; something.

Because I had a job again and went to AA, my parents agreed to pay first and last months' rent on an apartment plus a move-in deposit. The apartment was nothing special. It had three rooms: a living room/kitchen, a bedroom and a barely existing bathroom. The tub, toilet and sink were crammed in like cans into a tight cupboard, and the toilet was right behind the door, which meant if there was any possibility I'd ever live with someone, he'd smash my kneecaps or at least dislocate them opening that door; or if I stood at the toilet to take a piss, this nonexistent man could easily take out my back and cripple me forever. Something like this would add injury to insult far as my parents went. An alcoholic son who was now also a cripple. Where would they put me? A place like Juniper but for cripples? Or a place where the residents developed bedsores because a person could lie there forever like the place was a goddamned morgue?

The apartment, at least, was better than rehab. Better than jail. At least nobody was looking at me and shaking his head, disappointed. I discovered, though, I could look in on my neighbors whose apartment window faced mine. There was only a short distance between us, a walkway and four feet of grass. Two guys lived in the other apartment. They looked like Eric Bana and Brad Pitt. Older guys: early thirties? Mostly, I saw them at night. I'd watch the one who looked like Brad Pitt cook dinner. He stood over a stove stirring a boiling pot of something, and the steam of that something would drift above his eyebrows, and he wore no shirt, the waist of his jeans was visible. He had an incredible stomach and chest and lean athletic arms. I'd watched them eat too. They had impeccable table manners. Their dining room table was circular. They sat by each other, like they probably bumped knees under the table, and sometimes the Eric Bana guy would laugh with such open-mouthed heartiness I wanted to cry at his tremendous display of joy.

Dinner was usually chicken or fish. I ate takeout or whatever was left over from takeout the night before and got into a habit of setting my chair in front of my window, then watching my neighbors eat while I sucked up greasy noodles from a Styrofoam container. After they finished eating, the guy who looked like Brad Pitt smoked a cigarette while his boyfriend did the dishes. I smoked with him. Everyone in AA smoked. What else could we do? After the Eric Bana guy finished the dishes, he leaned down to hug the other guy in his seat. One night they locked lips in an intense kiss. I was sure I saw tongue. Truthfully, I'd never seen anything like their kiss before. It began rough then softened then increased in intensity again, lips mashed and noses bumping, and they each grabbed hold of the other's head, and the Brad Pitt guy licked a circle around his boyfriend's mouth while the Eric Bana guy curled his fingers around his lover's ear. They let go. Exchanged a few words. Disappeared from my view. And I couldn't stand up from my chair for five minutes.

I kept every kid's room in Juniper House clean. At least for an hour after I left, their rooms were in order and no longer smelled of piss or rotting food stuffed in corners. I straightened pillows. Retrieved teddy bears. Opened curtains to let the sun in.

One day, this boy Ricky sat in a corner of his room looking at his hands. I went over, crouched beside him, and then tried to see around to his face. He stared at his hands without blinking and muttered while he wriggled and bent his fingers.

"Hey Ricky, you conjuring a magical spell?" *To make him normal enough he could live in the real world with his parents.*

I put my hands in his hair. His scalp felt hot. His hair was the softest thing I'd ever touched. Ricky began to scream and flail his arms around until they ended up wound up his thin opaque body like tether ball rope around a pole. I fell backward on my hands, then crab-walked away from him. A nurse rushed into the room.

"What did you do? Did you touch Ricky? Don't ever touch Ricky."

I sat in a chair in front of my window and jerked off. No lights, no curtains, just me shrouded in secrecy, my cock in my hand, and my neighbors over there visible through their living room window. They weren't doing anything special; they sat on their couch, side by side, and watched TV. Once in a while, the one who looked like Eric Bana scratched the side of his head. What if I went over there, what if I went over there right now? My dick hurt. My dick hurt so bad it killed me, looking at the two of them like that. I closed my eyes, focusing on my cock in my hands, and then when I opened them for one more look before I shot off, they weren't there. And I panicked. They'd gotten up, killed the lights, maybe gone to bed. I let go of my cock, which was still hard, and my balls felt incredibly swollen. I pulled on a jacket and went out. I felt like I walked funny, hunched over, in pain. I stood on the walkway a minute, then crossed into the grass visibly green in the moonlight. No light from their apartment. Seriously, my gut hurt. I crossed the grass, hands in my jacket pockets. When I reached the window, I lifted my hands, then pressed them to the glass. I sucked in a breath then exhaled. Hi, hi, hi. Where were they? Just a glimpse: that was all I needed. I felt desperate. Locked out. On edge. What if I broke in while they weren't home and stood in the middle of their kitchen, then went to the stove and turned on a burner, held my hand to the heat, close as I could, then opened the fridge and drank from a carton of milk? Drank all of their milk? Maybe I'd find some hair in a bathroom drain, pinch a few strands between my fingers, and then push the strands into my pocket. I could go through their drawers, their laundry basket, the garbage cans, make treasure from trash. I could lie on their bed and jerk off. What if I took a Polaroid of myself on their bed jerking off?

All of a sudden, it felt important to at least hear them fuck in there: heavy breathing, bedsprings, maybe a headboard hitting a wall. I crept to what I knew was a bedroom window and then pressed the side of my face to the glass and strained my ear. Nothing. Wait, maybe a bedspring. I pretended I saw the one who looked like Brad Pitt getting behind the one who looked like Eric Bana. A huff of breath. Another squeaking bedspring. I wanted to see their male bodies naked and marblelike, slippery and sliding off each other in a glow from a single light. I wanted them to turn a light on. Please! I wanted to see one with his ass in the air. The other gripping him by the hips. I wanted to experience their fucking. I pushed my hand to my crotch. My boner flinched. Pre-come in my pants. I peered into the bedroom window. Not even a shift of shadow.

Soon as I stepped away from their window, I couldn't go home. I walked to Eugene's apartment. He'd told me where he lived; less than eight blocks away. Soon as I got there, I pushed my way into the apartment. Eugene said, "Whoa," and then smiled. His ears appeared to wave at me in an eerie splash of light from his TV.

I bit one of his earlobes and tasted salt before cool metal. Eugene shuddered against me, then put his hands on my hips, moving around to my back and moving them up and down, squeezing my ass. His TV sent surreal echoes of silver light into the room, across his face, distorting—even disguising—his cysts.

"Will you suck me off?" I said.

Behind me I felt for a wall, then leaned against it. Eugene went to his knees. I rolled my eyes to the ceiling. Eugene yanked my button-fly open, dug his hands into my pants, and then came up with my cock. His palm felt sticky as an asshole around me, and I moved my hips to push my cock thorough his fist.

I pretended I was fucking the Brad Pitt guy, then his boyfriend.

"I didn't think I'd see you like this again," I heard Eugene say. His breath washed over the head of my cock. "This is a terrific surprise."

I was glad the TV was on; the sound drowned his voice out a little.

I took Bruce for a walk the next day. Outside Juniper House there was a circular walk lined by benches and grass and trees. We were supposed to direct the kids in one direction, never against the flow of traffic. Bruce walked ahead of me saying, "Hi, hi, hi." Above us in a tree, a bird flapped its wings then whistled. Bruce stopped. I stopped behind him, keeping my hands in my pockets, watching sunlight hit the back of his head.

The bird whistled again.

Bruce raised his hand then opened his fingers. I stared at light shining through them. "I've no idea how long this streak of responsibility will last, Bruce. What if I wake up tomorrow and can't say no to a twelve-pack? What if I feel like I'll die without booze? Sometimes I feel so fucking lame. What if I've made no progress at all?"

"Bird," Bruce said.

First thing I noticed that night as I sat in my chair at the window eating a salad I'd thrown together from stuff I'd bought at a grocery store, was the Eric Bana guy across from his boyfriend at the circular table. They shoveled food in their mouths while looking down at their plates. Pretty soon, the Brad Pitt guy stood up from his chair. I stopped eating. His boyfriend said something, and I could tell from the twist to his mouth the words were biting. The Brad Pitt guy turned his back to his boyfriend, and I sat forward in my seat. The Eric Bana guy said something else. He yelled it. I couldn't make out the words. The

Brad Pitt guy went as if to leave the room, but his boyfriend got in his way. They locked hands, got into a pushing match. The Brad Pitt guy struggled. His boyfriend held on. I imagined the sounds of grunting. Then the Brad Pitt guy finally shoved his boyfriend out of the way.

The Eric Bana guy stood where he was, and then he sank into his chair at the table. He pushed his plate away. A minute later, he put his head in his hands. My heart sped up. He stood up from his chair and flew from the room. Where were they? I rushed out of the apartment and stood on the lawn. A light in their bedroom came on and I rushed over, tripping on my own feet. I stood by the window, panting. I could feel my heart working blood through my veins. Then I peered into the window. Nothing. I craned my neck. I'd begun to sweat. There, I saw them. The Eric Bana guy sat on the end of the bed, his back to me. The Brad Pitt guy stood in front of him. Then his boyfriend stood, went to move past him, but the Brad Pitt guy grabbed him and held on. His boyfriend turned. They appeared to lock eyes. Then the Brad Pitt guy mouthed something. *I love you,* he said. Something urgent lodged in my throat. They pressed their foreheads together, holding each other around the shoulders, and stood that way illuminated by light.

Back inside my apartment, the phone rang. It was a foreign sound, maybe Mom. Thing was, could I talk to her? I just about let it ring too long before I picked up.

"Cam?" I heard a voice say.

"Yeah?"

"It's Eugene."

"Oh." Outside my window, all dark.

"What are you doing?"

What was I doing? "Nothing much."

"Want to hang out?"

"Was there an AA meeting tonight?" I tried to remember.

"There's always an AA meeting," he said. "I didn't go."

"Why not?"

"I'm not off the wagon or anything, just didn't want to go."

"Who's your sponsor?"

"Melissa. Who's yours?"

"I don't remember his name. Oh yeah, Kurt. I think he's friends with that Jeremy Johnson guy."

"Yeah, they hang out. So you definitely won't consider the newsletter?"

"I don't know."

"I think you should do it."

"I don't know."

"So want to hang out?"

"And do what? Like sex?"

"No. I mean, I'd like to, but we don't have to do that."

"Yeah," I said.

"Yeah, what? You want to hang out?"

"Yeah," I said again, and then I gave him directions to my apartment.

Not until I'd hung up did it occur to me I'd never done that before, given anyone directions to where I lived.

Eugene had gelled his hair again but not quite as obviously as before. He wore new jeans and a green T-shirt. He didn't look so bad, I thought.

"Want a drink? I have...milk and water, oh and a couple root beers."

"Yeah, sure. Root beer's good. It's hard, huh?"

"What is?" I opened the fridge and took out the sodas.

"Not drinking," he said.

I came back with the root beers. "Yeah." I handed him a can.

"Thanks." He cracked it open, then said, "I want a beer so bad right now."

I looked at him. "Really?"

"Hell yeah. I want a beer all the time, don't you?"

"Yeah, I guess so." I didn't look at him as I sat on the couch.

"It's okay, Cam. Seriously."

"What is?"

"That we want to drink."

I lifted the root beer to my mouth and then swallowed a bunch of carbonated syrup. Yeah, it would have been better if it had alcohol in it.

"Why did you drink?" he asked me.

"Why'd you?"

"Wow, okay, well, it was very cliché."

"What do you mean?" I studied his face. He was probably blushing.

"To feel like I fit in," Eugene said. "Like I said, totally cliché." He lifted his soda can and drank so long I thought he might drown himself. When he finally set it down he covered his mouth to burp and then said, "Sorry."

I shrugged. Eugene smiled. I felt myself smile too, which was weird, because I hadn't expected to do that.

"You're the first person who's been cool to me the whole time I've been here," I said.

Quiet. Then Eugene said, "Same here."

Wonder who looked in on us as I reached for his hand?

WILD NIGHT

Simon Sheppard

O San Francisco, city of horny ghosts...

Nobody likes a sentimental old fool, I suppose. And nostalgia, as the saying goes, ain't what it used to be. But let me tell you (anyway) that yes, it was good to be young and horny way back in the 1970s—before gentrification, before HIV, before the death of dreams.

The Castro? The Castro was where you went to dance, to drink, and, in the early days, to hang out with the Cockettes after hours at the all-night donut shop. Though if you *did* crave quick cock, there was Jaguar Books, with its makeshift upstairs orgy room: hand over a mere twenty-five cents at the turnstile and it was just a short climb to something like ecstasy. And if something just a little grander was on the bill, the 1808 Club, six blocks away on Market Street, offered a maze of glory holes for Castro-area cocksuckers.

But if Eighteenth and Castro was the intersection of a burgeoning queer community, the town's throbbing libido was based a little lower down, south of Market Street, South of the Slot. Down on Folsom Street.

I was young then, of course, and temporal distance lends enchantment. But I truly think it's true: on those few gritty blocks bloomed a garden of earthly delights, a cock-filled cornucopia redolent of Weimar at its wildest, Sodom before the brimstone, Eden before the Fall.

Back then I was also, in my peculiarly jaded way, innocent... or at least inhibited. There were places, scenes, where I never set foot. There was the Cauldron, where "water sports" had nothing to do with surfing. And the Slot, where men fisted each other, a pursuit that seemed so anatomically improbable that when I first heard about it, I dismissed it as an urban myth...but no, it turned out that all it took was a bottle of poppers, some patience, and a glob of Crisco. And there was also the Catacombs, a dungeon so depraved, it was whispered, that the Slot was a convent by comparison.

(I did make it at least to the front desk of the Slot, where a boyfriend of mine worked as a towel boy. It is, I suppose, a minor-but-lasting regret of mine that that's as far as I ever went.)

So, heavy kink was beyond my ken. I did, however, patronize a few of the more mundane penis-palaces. I got down on my knees in the misty precincts of the Ritch Street Baths' tiled steam room, thrusting my tongue into the nether regions of a half-seen muscle-hunk, thereby contracting a positively gruesome case of shigellosis (though not even that erased my taste for rimming). The Bulldog Baths, down on Turk Street in the seamy Tenderloin, featured—if memory serves—the cab of a semi truck plunked down, shining headlights and all, in the middle of a rather butch orgy room, as well as a two-story cell block, a novelly transgressive mise-en-scène for the same old sodomy. The Twenty-first Street Baths, nearest bathhouse to the

Castro district, was airy and uncontrived by comparison.

And I once paid a visit to the Sutro Baths, the city's only coed bathhouse; the men were mostly heterosexual, the women decidedly outnumbered, and I dimly recall giving head to a very cute boy, who might or might not have been bisexual but in any case made the visit well worthwhile. I also remember a campout room, with tents set up in a dimly lit space achirp with the piped-in calls of crickets, an invitation to sex in the great faux outdoors. On second thought, that campout room might have been somewhere else; it's been quite a while. (But hey, this is a love letter, not a grand tour.)

Still, the bathhouses, however fabulous, however hot the action (and who can ever forget the sight of that famous fister with his arm sunk improbably deep into another man, only to pull it out and reveal he was an amputee?), for all their sometimes-deluxe and always lust-filled ambience, ran second place in my affections to San Francisco's infamous backroom bars.

Now there are those—queer men amongst them—who decry recreational sex. Just the other day, cruising for action on Craigslist, I ran across a posting by a no doubt splendid fellow who insisted that we gay guys grow up, stop fucking around, and take our rightful places as properly partnered monogamous men, preferably with rugrats in tow.

Sure, responsibility has its upside. And, if I'm honest with myself, I'll have to fess up that I've wasted an uncountable number of hours in the pursuit of more-or-less random orgasms. When I should have been studying graphic design at City College, for instance, I often as not took a sex-filled study break in the men's room. On the other hand, all the techniques I learned back in the era of X-Acto and hot wax layouts are as obsolete as blacksmithing, but I still recall that blond in the bulky white sweater who was my very first tearoom trick.

And heaven knows the action in the balcony of the Strand Theater kept me entertained through any number of execrable double features. It was, yes, a formative experience for me to get blown during the battle scenes of *Young Winston*, though the long-gone theater's balcony, with its sticky floors, scampering rodents, and dozing junkies, now seems as long-ago and far-off as the Boer War.

Somewhere along the line, I'm sure I visited at least one of the provocatively titled "adult theaters" in the always-gamey Tenderloin—the Circle J? The Tearoom?—where classic raincoat-on-the-lap mutual hand jobs were fitfully illuminated by the glow of grainy porn "loops." And I dimly recall visiting the Church of Priapus, a sodomitical sanctuary where, in my flawed memory at least, the "services" were held in a grungy apartment reeking of cat pee. Ah, those were indeed the days.

And the nights.

After dark, you see, lust ran wild at wide-open San Francisco's sex bars. In those days, before the Internet made getting laid as potentially easy as ordering out for pizza (and too often as frustrating as hell), a night at the backroom bars was perhaps the simplest, safest path to getting one's rocks more-or-less off. And, unlike going to the baths, stopping by a bar for a blow was an impromptu, low-commitment affair; the borderline between a beer at the pub and public sex was permeable indeed.

I recall the feelings of anticipation as I alighted from the Muni bus and headed down some dimly lit street in what was then still a rather industrial part of the city, a neighborhood where faggots and funkiness had not yet been supplanted by het fashionistas strutting their stuff at bridge-and-tunnel boîtes. Heading down the sidewalk toward expected stand-up sex, humming

Van Morrison's "Wild Night" to myself, I felt so very naughty, so much more sleazily mature than I'd been when I first moved to San Francisco and settled into a gay hippie commune not far from Golden Gate Park, a delightfully drug-soaked place where Sylvester and the other Cockettes would come to call, and where I rather successfully kicked over the traces of my well-behaved middle-class upbringing.

Okay, I still wasn't nearly as rakish as I thought I was. Yes, I went to the weekly slave auctions at the Arena bar, but mostly to see Mister Marcus fling embarrassing questions at nearly naked contestants who, when commanded to, readily bent over to display their well-used holes. I had very little idea, though, of what actually went on once the slaves were taken home by the Masters who'd successfully bid for them; it would be another decade or longer before I learned to swing a flogger and properly degrade tied-up bottomboys. Poor me.

My still-vanilla nature didn't stop me, however, from hanging out at the Black and Blue, where, if fading memory serves, a gleaming motorcycle hung suspended over the pool table and a semisecluded little corner alcove provided cover for cocksucking.

There was, too, the even more suavely monikered Hungry Hole. I'm sure I hung out there, I'm sure that I swallowed gallons of what porn writer Dirk Vanden dubbed "someone's unborn children," but I'll be damned if I remember a single thing about the place. Except the name. And though the orgy room at the hyperbutch Ambush had a popper-soaked notoriety that approached the status of legend, I have no memory of playing there, either. Maybe the chaps-and-chains ambience intimidated me. Or maybe I was too stoned at the time for memories to stick.

I do vividly recall the back room at Folsom Prison, even though it was pitch black, save a single dim red bulb somewhere ceilingward. That was a venue for venery at its most anonymous, where touch, taste, and smell were all you had to go on. On a good night, bounties of sweaty flesh—indistinguishable as its owners might have been in that Stygian, popper-infused gloom—fused the transcendent and the trashy and the true.

Best of all, though, was the Boot Camp, where the back room was in fact in the front room, an orgiastic area partitioned off from the bar by nothing more than a few oil drums. I still remember—or at least *think* I remember, which is pretty much the same thing, really—one stand-up fuck, my bottomboy perched on a bench while I plowed away, as one of the breakthrough booty moments of my life.

If you are, like me, one of the fortunate ones who slutted around back then and still managed to survive, then you most likely have your own memories, your own favorite dives, too. Ah, where is the sperm of yesteryear?

Okay, sure, I was looking for love—a love I was shortly to find in an enduring, endearingly open relationship that is, I'm thrilled to note, still going strong. But that search for affection didn't preclude the call of those wild nights, that quest for meaningless, objectified, endlessly lovely male-to-male (to-male-to-male-to-male, sometimes) sex. Because San Francisco was, as it had always been, about adventure, possibility, the gilded bacchanal. Or at least so the myth goes.

And then came the crash, part, as it happened, of one of the greatest health crises in the history of humankind. Okay, nobody saw it coming. But even if, as Prince has pointed out, parties weren't made to last, this particular orgy wound down especially quickly and brutally, with a sickening viral thud.

We all know the story. The butch boys and fabulous fisters started dropping like flies. In, tellingly, 1984, then-mayor

Dianne Feinstein shut down the bathhouses...which, truth be told, had not been all that proactive in the face of oncoming plague. Folsom Street became a ghost town, Castro Street an outpatient ward. Larry Kramer kvetched at us. Homocon Andrew Sullivan castigated us for being immature and irresponsible, even while he was secretly cruising for bareback sex. We were goaded to disavow sex, drugs, and rock and roll, unless they were, respectively: in the context of a committed relationship; Viagra; and the Clash's soundtrack to a Jaguar ad.

In the bedraggled City by the Bay, sex took a decided nosedive. Defunct backroom bars and bathhouses were supplanted by no-private-cubicles sex clubs, from the clean and well-lighted Eros, to Mike's Night Gallery, which was neither. The hospital overlooking Buena Vista Park was turned into pricey condos, the neighbors began complaining about hanky-panky in the underbrush, and defoliation followed. The overgrown paths at Land's End—where I'd screwed a dog-walking redhead slung over a log while his pooch waited patiently—fell under the supervision of the National Park Service, and families replaced fucking. And, lest we forgot and got a hard-on, the walking wounded of Castro Street served as a memento mori: Not only silence equaled death. Sex did, too.

Yet, even amongst the trendy restaurants and trendier nightspots, and even amidst the plague, South-of-Market sex in bars persisted. There was the dangerously crowded patio of the Powerhouse. And, sleaziest of all, My Place, a hangout for pervs from every walk of life, from tweaked hipsters to closeted husbands; like the Strand Theater before it, My Place epitomized the great democracy of dick. And let's not even *talk* about what took place at the urinal trough. Sure, the bar was engaged in a running battle with the powers that be, which led to some odd regulations: once I was reprimanded by a barback who told me I could fuck my friend in the back of the bar, but only if his trousers remained up around his thighs. Go figure. Eventually, the state's Department of Alcoholic Beverage Control got its way and permanently shut the joint down, and then there were none. More or less.

Now the Strand stands shuttered on Market Street, awaiting the wrecking ball. A discount supermarket has been built on the site of Folsom Prison, while the Black and Blue's former home now houses, chromatically enough, a paint store. Folsom Street Barracks bathhouse, destroyed in a massive 1981 fire, has been replaced by a het-yuppie bar serving microbrewery beers. And where the Boot Camp reigned, there's now a Chinese restaurant. At 1808 Market Street there stands the chastely welcoming GLBT Community Center, apparently unhaunted despite being built over untold orgasms' graveyard. At least the Arena was succeeded by the relocated Stud, the city's original hippie-stoner bar, which didn't host sex, but did feature Yoko Ono on the jukebox.

But hey, it's no use crying over spilled sperm. Some sage pointed out that the very best rock and roll was made when you were eighteen—no matter when you were born. Nope, things aren't what they used to be. And they never were. Still, I can't help but wonder whether, in some globally warmed future, some aging pornographer will look back on the Arctic Monkeys and cruising Craigslist with the same unforgivably sloppy sentimentality I reserve for the Velvet Underground and wild nights at the Boot Camp.

I know, I know. The struggle for queer liberation comes down to much more than a furtive blow job in the dark. Of course, of course. And times change. New HIV treatments have brought some of us, like lecherous Lazaruses, up from the brink of the grave and back down on our knees. Folsom, despite its annual S/M street fair, may be a pale shadow of its former raunchy self, but the Castro is vibrant again, even if there's a Pottery Barn hovering above its now-unaffordable precincts. Guys still gather for group fucks at places ranging from the Citadel to the Faerie House. And if barebacking and crystal meth are inviting the Angel of Death to stick around for a while, if desperate men still search for love and find ashes instead, if an endless quest for penis can be, in point of fact, rather problematical...well, there have been quite enough threnodies, thank you very much. Too many, in fact.

Because even now, even at the very moment you're reading this sentence, somewhere or other in San Francisco, two men who have just met are naked before each other, erect, and for one long orgasmic moment, everything is, for them, joyful and beautiful and right.

Same as it was at the Boot Camp on some long-ago dark, wild night.

HALF-LIFE

Dale Chase

It's something the doctor says. In with admonishments toward better habits, good diet, and reduced stress comes a throw-away line that jabs me like another needle. "While you're at it," the doc says as he turns to leave, "take a look at what's underneath."

He doesn't wait for a reply, probably because he knows men are reluctant to explore the underpinnings, especially when it smells down there. I shut my eyes and feel the ooze begin to rise. The heart monitor takes note with a faster beat.

ICU is not a good place to be at forty-eight. Captive with mortality, the pain of both the heart attack and emergency angioplasty still fresh, I am caught in a muzzle of gratitude and fear. Dr. Robbins says I've "stabilized," assures me the worst is over, yet as I lie here and allow what's underneath I almost want to laugh because stable I will never be.

Relax, I tell myself. *Rest. Recover.* I try to let go of all thought and for a few seconds it almost works but the audible beep of my heart reminds me this isn't some leisurely summer afternoon and who in hell can relax when his heart has failed?

My mind is always too busy and maybe that's part of the problem, that hit-the-ground-running that starts when I open my eyes each morning. It never really lets up unless I focus on something—usually work but sometimes other things. Men, actually. Men. A familiar twinge rolls from spine to crotch and I remind myself to stay calm even as my hand slides down between my legs.

My wants are clear yet complicated. From the distant past I call up the weight of a cock on my tongue, the feel of the thing as I trace the shaft and finally close around the knob to suck. I pull on my limp dick as the climax replays but I don't get hard. I know it's the heart thing, trussed up as I am here with wires and machines, full of blood thinners. *So stop thinking about it.* Maureen will be here soon with plans for my recovery: low-fat diet, long walks. I see us on the nature trail, side by side in our fleece and it's a cold fall day but then my butt is up and he's got his dick in me, fucking my ass, and I'm creaming in the sheets and going ballistic, begging him to do it, *Fuck me, fuck me—*

"Mr. Cahill?"

My eyes pop open, my breath catches. A nurse stands over me, the bedside beep having summoned her. "What are you feeling?" she asks. "Are you in pain?"

I can't speak. My chin quivers because I can't tell her I'm in the middle of a mind-fuck and would she get the hell out.

"Mr. Cahill," she says, alarm in her tone.

"No, I'm fine," I manage. "Bad dream. It's nothing. I'm fine, really."

"Are you in pain?"

"No."

But I am, of course, awakening here in the ICU. Before, it was something undefined, skating along on a cushion of malaise, but now there's a smell down there and I crave it deeply.

The nurse fusses over me a bit more, then retreats with a skeptical eye. *Don't think of men,* I tell myself, and then Maureen arrives.

She is loving and attentive; I am receptive and appropriate. We are well practiced, after all. As I listen to her news I think about a cock in me. My hand is still on my dick.

She stays the afternoon, then tells me her friend Jan is taking her to dinner to cheer her up. I am enthusiastic because I do care. I also want her gone.

When I'm alone, dark coming on, I carefully revisit my life but Maureen trails along like some little sister and I allow it for maybe a minute, because I dare not give it more than that, what it would be were I unstuck. I see the cock; I see myself turn and bend. When I get out of here all I'm going to do is fuck.

Next day I'm moved to the cardiac care unit where I'm attended by a handsome young Latino who has no idea I'm interested in what's in his pants. While he tells of a brother-in-law also felled with a heart attack, now fully recovered and stronger than ever, I keep my hand on my dick, which gives me a modest thrill. The situation is amusing in a depressing sort of way.

Convalescence is an awful word, old sounding, but that's what I descend into. *Recovery* is no better, tainted with addiction. Whatever, the six weeks are long and tedious as I confront my life without the escape of work. Maureen is efficient, as I knew she would be. We embark on the low-fat diet, we walk and walk. We talk more than ever—about the kids, the house, life in general—and it's as we reach the three mile point on the trail one day and turn back to retrace our steps that I allow that I don't want this life anymore. It's not a bad life but it doesn't have to be a bad life, just the wrong life. Like I detoured early and never got back to the main track. A half life rather than a whole.

Maureen is talking about our oldest son, Andy, who's in his second year at USC and I'm agreeing but the long-suppressed part of me inches toward the ooze. When a jogger approaches, in his thirties maybe, in shorts and tee, my body awakens and for the few seconds he passes I consider what's in those shorts. My dick starts to fill and I want to bare my ass here and now and do it. *Fuck me, for god's sake, fuck me.* When he's gone I switch back on automatic, become more animated with Maureen.

I haven't fucked her since the heart attack and she understands and I play on that even as I jerk off in the shower to thoughts of sex with faceless men. I see a line of hard cocks. When one finishes, I bend for another.

Middle of week five I give way. While Maureen plays tennis I sit at the computer and wade into possibility on Craigslist. I've always kept myself from such indulgence so I know this is part of the heart thing, mortality reordering priorities, but who cares in the face of the offers? Some are more demands—*Come over and fuck me right now.* I free my dick as I read, work myself to a frenzy and spray jizz into a wad of Kleenex.

Returning to work has a surreal quality. I experience a disconnected some-other-guy feeling, accepting welcomes as I make my way to my office. Like a third-party observer, I become acutely aware of every move, every gesture. Opening a drawer I note my hand is the one I wrap around my dick to get off. Starting my computer, I think of the bounty of Craigslist. At the ten o'clock sales meeting I accept kind words, jostling fun, but as I try to reconnect with what I do for a living I still feel once removed. I also find a certain relief at being out of this particular loop; nobody expects input from me due to the long absence. I fix my eyes on my notepad and tell myself to role-play for a while, act my life until I get the hang of it again, but then I hear a familiar voice. It's Tim Silvey, the new guy. I slowly look up.

Tim is single, thirty-two, and gay. His sandy good looks and quiet energy captured me from day one and have since kept me stuck like some bug pinned to a board. He's got a wonderful warm low-key sort of animation, highly personable and thus a born salesman. Everybody likes him. As he speaks of business I experience an awful rush. My heart begins to pound, my cock to stiffen, which forces me to admit this is where my near-demise began. I want this man so much it's painful. I look down at my yellow lined pad where my hand grips the pen in near desperation.

Sweat breaks out across my forehead as Tim cedes the floor to others. A spirited discussion of sales strategy ensues and where I'd usually jump in, I retreat. My mouth goes dry; my throat starts closing up. I rise, excuse myself with as much calm as I can muster, keeping the yellow pad in front of me to hide the erection. In the bathroom I hurry into a stall because I want privacy but once there I'm lost. Is it my heart or my mind? Am I terribly sick or terribly well?

"Keith?"

It's Tim and I don't know what to say. I can't even acknowledge myself and maybe that's most telling.

"You okay in there?" he asks.

"Yes," I rasp.

"That doesn't sound okay. Is it your heart or maybe some anxiety? I can understand that, six weeks away then dumped into barracuda central. C'mon, come out of there, talk to me."

I am seated because it's what you do in here unless you're jerking off, which I did a lot those last weeks and oh god this is hell. I am coming unglued but my dick is still hard and that's how they'll find the body. "Well would you look at that," one paramedic will say to another. "Dick still up and him gone."

"Keith," Tim says. "I'm not going away."

When I don't respond, he tells me what I need to hear, what I have needed to hear since he first walked in the door three months ago. "You know, I feel it too. The attraction is mutual, okay?"

Mutual. I seize on the word, my mind undone. Mutual masturbation, mutual fund, our competitor Provident Mutual. The word runs laps inside my head until I unlatch the door. Tim pushes it open but doesn't join me. "Everybody's concerned," he says, which is not what I want to hear and he sees this. "Especially me," he adds.

"I want to go to my office," I tell him. "Forget the meeting, just be quiet for a while."

"Sure. Can you get up?"

I look into warm brown eyes. "I don't know. Pretty shaky." Except in my cock where my entire blood supply has apparently pooled. Sex is the last thing I want right now but tell that to a dick. Tim takes my arm, I rise to him, and we stand there in the stall doorway for a few seconds, allowing the thing that exists between us. It's the best I've felt in six weeks.

I splash cold water over my face, rejoice in reinvigoration. My breathing calms; everything settles. A limp dick has never been so welcome. Tim remains nearby and as I mop up he suggests we meet for a drink after work. "Sit and talk awhile."

"You know I'm married," I blurt.

"I know."

"Okay then."

We work in Walnut Creek, an upscale suburb twenty miles east of San Francisco and five miles north of Danville, the even more upscale bedroom community where I live. "How about La Tapitia?" Tim says. "Great margaritas."

I nod. "I'm sorry about all this."

"Don't be. It's okay. See you at five?"

"See you then."

"You okay to get back to your office?"

"Yes. I'm surprisingly fine."

He smiles, gives me a playful punch on the shoulder, and leaves. I make my way to my office, joking with concerned co-workers that I should have known better than to start with a sales meeting. In my office I shut the door, sit at my desk, and turn toward a view I seldom notice: Mount Diablo with greater Walnut Creek at its feet, elevated BART tracks cutting in front, cars down on Main Street. It all looks new.

Gradually I embrace what is happening even as I'm not sure exactly what that is. Meeting Tim to talk, yes, but what about? Is he getting me off-site so I won't make a scene when he tells me he doesn't date married men? Or men he works with? Is he going to explain how he's a San Francisco guy who happens to work over here so his life is more there than here and I'm just too suburban? Or maybe he has a lover. Oh shit, I never thought of that but then I never really thought at all. Resist was all I ever did. Partner. That's what it is now. Maybe he's got a partner and they fucked this morning and he's not about to do the middle-aged married guy.

It takes minutes to make myself miserable and the rest of the day to talk my way out of it. When I head for La Tapitia shortly before five, I feel an exhausted kind of elation, which is probably best.

Tim is already there, pitcher of margaritas in front of him, and when I sit he pours me one. As we lift our drinks he says, "Welcome back."

A waitress materializes. "Can I get you gentlemen some appetizers?"

Tim looks at me like we do this all the time. "Chips and salsa?"

I nod, realizing the girl thinks were a couple. This makes me giddy, embarrassed. I break into a smile.

"That's what I like to see," Tim says. "You feeling better?"

I blow out a long sigh. "Much, thanks to you." There's more but I sip my drink instead. Licking salt off my lips, glancing at Tim, I feel suddenly empowered. "You know, the whole episode had a lot to do with you," I say. "Nothing negative on your part, don't get me wrong. It was all me...but...centered on you. Those months before, when you first arrived..."

He's locked on to me now and I struggle for a second, then press on. "Those months were agony, trying to hold back."

"I had no idea."

"Well, I didn't want you to. I mean the last thing I wanted was to be coming on to a guy who's not interested and I wouldn't know how anyway. God, I'm just some ruin."

"I don't see you that way at all."

"No?"

He shakes his head so slowly it's a come-on in itself. "What I do see is an attractive older guy trying to contain his desire and the levee finally gave way."

"He nearly drowned."

The chips and salsa arrive but we hardly notice. I'm aware of restaurant sounds—clinking glasses, the hum of conversation—but they're mere accompaniment to what is taking place between us. I sip my drink and he does his, our eyes meeting over the glasses. I'm aroused again but for once it's okay and I savor the feel of a dick that's hard for the man sitting across from me.

"Want to come to my place?" Tim says.

I nod and tell him I have to call my wife. "Is that a problem?" he asks.

I don't care if it is but I don't say this. "No, shouldn't be."

I take out my phone hoping she doesn't pick up and mercifully she doesn't. "Hi honey. Some of the guys are taking me to dinner so I'll see you later and I know, take it easy. Don't worry, I will. Don't wait up." I know I'm doing her a terrible wrong but can't help it because what I'm going to do feels so terribly right.

Tim downs the rest of his drink, motions for the check. We are soon on the train to San Francisco, my car left in Walnut Creek. I ask Tim about his place, get him talking about the city I've denied myself. Question after question until I finally laugh. "You'd never know I live in the Bay Area, would you, but I don't get to San Francisco that much. Plays, the symphony. Your world is foreign to me." He assures me he understands.

We exit the train at Embarcadero and take a cable car up to Polk, then walk four blocks to his building. Polk Street is like a different country and I savor the eclectic mix of character and grunge. Tim lives in a well-maintained, skinny, twenties-era five-story building. It has the smallest elevator I've ever seen, and it's here that he begins. He's already hit the button for five when he presses himself to me. As we start rumbling upward, he kisses me, hard cock against mine. I open to his tongue, which is voracious, as is his grinding below. I am beside myself with arousal, humping like some mad ape when a bell rings and the car lurches to a stop. Tim pulls off like he's well practiced at interruptions while I'm lost, caught between floors so to speak. "C'mon," he says with a grin and I follow him about three feet to his door, which is next to the elevator. In seconds it's opened and closed and we're in a colorful studio apartment with a bicycle in the entry, an easel in the corner, and colorful abstract art on the walls. As he kneels to undo my pants and get out my cock, I take in the scenery, probably because where I am doesn't feel at all real. And even when he's got a hand on my dick I'm still oddly disconnected, watching the scene, trying to gain a foothold. I look down and he looks up as he opens his mouth. I watch him guide me in.

I shoot like some seventh-grader. Frantic as he sucks the spunk out of me, I grab his head because I have to hold on to something. I can't help but thrust, such is the torrent. Grunts and slurping and moans and the faint rush of traffic roll into a great ocean of sound and then there's my conscious thought, which keeps shouting, "I'm there! I'm fucking there!"

When I'm empty Tim doesn't pull off right away. He diddles my softy, reaches under for my balls, then past them. A finger skates my hole and I flinch.

"Easy," he says, like I'm some skittish horse. "Easy."

He leaves my anxious pucker long enough to wet the finger, then returns, prods. I manage a yes and he pushes in, which makes me squirm and he gets the idea, sticks it in all the way, palm plastered on my ass. "Oh yeah," he says as I ride the digit.

When he pulls out I'm totally lost. I want him in me but all I can do is flail about. "Easy," he says again. "Undress. Get on the bed."

He pulls back the covers and while I strip he gets stuff from the nightstand: condoms, lube, whatever's needed these days. Then he undresses.

I sit on the edge of the bed feeling almost too naked as he reveals himself. He's hairier than me, curly brown across a nicely defined chest. I see nipples in the fur, think how I can get my mouth on them but first I want what he's got below.

His dick is average and cut, a lot like mine. It's also hard and drooling. When he's naked he starts to stroke it. "Stretch out," he says and I lie on my back. He climbs on top of me.

"I have wanted you since day one," he tells me. "Remember how Finstrom was going on about all your experience and how you could teach me so much and I'm thinking *I'd like to teach him something*. You're so fucking sexy, Keith." And with that begins the most true and complete sexual experience I've ever known.

Where I expect to be rolled over and fucked, Tim surprises me by taking it slow. As his lips and tongue move from mouth to ear to throat, I allow my hands to slide onto his butt, to rub and knead, all the while his slippery cock between us. His hips move like he's already fucking and it drives me crazy. All the years and sex was nothing like this.

He looks up at me finally and I want to say things, how much it all means, how good it feels, but then he's easing down to get that tongue onto my chest. I've never had my tits licked and I'm moaning, pushing at him and he responds, nibbles at the little nubs, which makes me start to beg. "Fuck me, please. I can't stand it. I want you in me."

He raises up, gets condom and lube without comment. I watch him prepare himself, thinking how it's all for me. Then he's rolling me over, pulling my ass up. He shoves gobs of grease into me and I about go nuts from just his finger. He's opening me, I know that much, because I'm tight back there, and when he adds a second finger it hurts but who cares? I push back at him like I want the whole fucking hand.

Once I'm ready I tuck my knees in and feel his hands on my butt. As he parts my cheeks his dick pokes at me, hits the center. Without comment, he pushes in. I let out a welcome cry.

As he begins an easy stroke, I am transported. It's what I've always craved. No more resistance. He's in me; he's fucking me.

I note everything about what's happening—feel, sound, reason. I think of him back there shoving it in, imagine him looking down to see his cock do it. I concentrate on my butthole fully occupied, accommodating his thrusting prick, and I see that this is where true pleasure lies.

"So good," I tell him.

In reply he rams into me and from then on he's more forceful. I hear him grunting back there, know the juice is stirring, balls boiling; he's ready to unload. "Give it to me," I tell him and he goes faster, fingers digging in as he pounds it out and then he's there and yells "I'm gonna" before it turns to your basic guttural gibberish. I picture his dick firing spunk. Into me.

When he's done and pulls out I roll over and watch him strip away the condom. It's tossed over the bedside as he falls forward. He's breathing heavily, sweat all across him. He lies facing me and I inhale the pungence. "I like that," I say. "The smell of sex."

He offers no reply and we settle into a bit of quiet in which I explore him. When my finger finds his tit he smiles, lets me rub and play, get my mouth on him. I feel the hard nub on my tongue, lick and bite, then finally just suck. I keep my eyes open because I want to see myself buried in this gorgeous man's chest.

We evolve from this point into an hours-long foreplay, each claiming the other. In addition to his tits, I suck his balls, delighted when he lies back and spreads his legs. After a while he raises his knees and I'm looking at his hairy butthole. I glance up, questioning, and he tells me to do what I want. "Give and take," he says. "I like it all."

I wet a finger and hesitate because I've never touched anyone there, not the guy in college, not Maureen. But I know how good it feels so I push into him, feel the spongy warmth, hear him moan. I look up to see his eyelids flutter.

I work him and he squirms just like I did. My dick is up now because this is so hot and I realize I'm going to fuck him up the ass. The possibility is almost too much. I start to gasp but don't care if it's another heart attack because I'm going to do this. As if to confirm my intent he utters "Fuck me."

I scramble for protection, hands shaking as I tear open the

condom packet. He watches me apply it, then says "lube." I grease myself and just about come running the stuff into him but then we're ready and he raises his legs high and clenches his muscle so the hole itself beckons. And I do it, honest-to-god I shove it in, and once there I cannot stop. I can't speak either, everything in me pooled in my dick again only this time with purpose and also a bit of madness. It becomes my all, the give and take. Fuck me; fuck you.

I don't last as long as I'd like but who cares when it's shooting into a guy's ass, a guy you like, a guy who's just fucked you? Christ, it's good and he strokes his dick as I do him, telling me "Fuck yeah" over and over until I let out a howl and the come shoots out of me and into him and I look down at his face, his eyes, because I want that connection too.

It's over, but not really. We lie entangled, tired, sweaty, and I tell him this and he gets it. Over does not apply to what is happening between us. Respite? Interlude?

Tim laughs. "Time out?"

Lying in his arms I need consider nothing beyond him and this is so new for me because I'm always thinking of the next thing while still in the present, whether work or sport or the rigors of marriage. There hasn't really been a stopping point and I've never seen this until now—because how can you see anything when you're always rushing because maybe, just maybe, you're afraid to stop. I'm shaking my head in wonder when Tim asks, "What?"

"I don't know, just stuff. Do you know I've never really stopped until now? I'm like some perpetual motion machine and maybe that's what's been wrong. It's so good to lie here and just be. You give me that."

He kisses my cheek. "My pleasure and you know, it's a two-way street."

I chuckle. "Like how?"

"I don't chase around a lot. I prefer something more stable, relationships instead of one-nighters. I'm way too domestic so when a man feels really right, like you do, I make myself known."

"So what we're saying..."

"Is we have something here."

I close my eyes because they're wet now and I don't want to get maudlin or mushy, even if that's how it feels. I'm stirred to the deepest core and it's so incredibly new, which brings both joy and sadness. All those years.

"Can you stay over?" Tim asks.

"I want to."

"But?"

"I'm expected home. I can call but what on earth do I say? I mean, how do I approach what's happening, because it's ultimately happening to her?"

Tim nods, ponders, then asks, "What'll happen when you go home?"

I open my eyes, let the tears run down my cheeks. "I don't want to think about that."

Tim gives it a few more seconds, then says, "You have to at some point."

"I know, I know, and it pisses me off if you want the truth. I've never felt trapped until now and you know why that is? Because we're over here fucking and she's over there waiting. Christ, it's impossible."

I hear my voice rising, feel my face flush. Tim says nothing and I sit up, suddenly uncontainable. "How do you tell someone it's all been a mistake? Sorry, wrong choice, never mind the kids and the house and the *life*. I don't want to hurt anybody but don't I get to stop hurting? But I'm the one who set the trap, aren't I? Laid it out there and stepped right in and now I'm going to have to chew off my foot to get free."

I stop to gather breath; I clench and unclench my fists. Tim sits up but remains silent as I resume the rant. "I have to tell her but I hate having to tell her, you know? I *hate* it! I am not a hurtful person but I have to hurt her—but how do I do it? 'Maureen, there's something you need to know,' or 'Maureen, I'm fucking a guy at the office,' or 'Maureen, you're a great wife but I like men.' There is no good way out."

I'm angry at myself for creating the situation and I hate that too, marriage reduced to situation. I tell Tim all this, feel it escalate inside me until he starts trying to calm me down and I pull away, leap out of bed like there's somewhere to go where none of it can follow. I'm even angry at Tim but don't know why and I'm sick of the questions, and more, of the answers.

I pace the room, naked madman consumed by predicament, and then Tim is at my elbow and I turn, shove him, then cry out, reach for him. I'm shaking; I have no control over any of it, trapped in some unearthly storm of my own making. I look at Tim, who walked into my life and turned it onto its side. I think of those first weeks, aroused by his proximity and thrilled by the arousal, working to get up close and distance myself at the same time. I feel the agony all over again, an urge so strong it came up in my throat like bile and I swallowed it down over and over until my insides couldn't take it anymore. I remember the bathroom, jerking off and practically throwing up at the same time.

"What?" Tim asks. He's in front of me, hands up like he's trying to corral me. "Tell me what's happening."

I can't speak. It's all there again; I wait for chest pains.

"What's going on?" Tim demands. He takes me by the shoulders, holds on. "What is it?"

"I remember that day, getting off in the bathroom because of you, I couldn't stand it, you were so close and my dick was hard and earlier that morning the New Jersey governor was on TV, outed because he'd been seeing this male hooker, and god how I hated him."

"Why would you hate him?"

"Because...because..."

"Why?"

"He just stood there and told everyone yes, he was gay, just like that."

"Why would you hate him for that?"

"I don't know but I was angry driving to work, really pissed with traffic, the garage, the elevator, everything going along like always when it wasn't anymore. Then you and all of the rest."

Tim eases me down onto the bed. We sit side by side. "Are you still angry?"

The question makes it reignite. "That's silly," I snap, then, "I don't know. Yeah, maybe."

"Why would that be?"

"I guess because that governor is out and I'm not."

"Is that all?"

I look at him, puzzled.

"Could it be," Tim says softly, "that you're angry because he didn't have to call his wife and tell her he's gay? Someone did it for him."

I'm repulsed, try to leap up but Tim holds me where I am. "No, no way," I insist. "No." But he's right, of course, and after a bit I slump against him. "That's pitiful."

"No, it's just human. The media did his confession for him while you have to go it alone."

I feel like I'm swimming behind another levee only this one hasn't yet burst. It's straining at the seams though and I cling to Tim, wishing it would just give way once and for all.

"I'm going to stay with you," I finally tell him. "I'll call home later."

"I'll make us some tea."

Tim puts on a robe, hands me another. We sit on stools at a tiny breakfast bar in his miniscule kitchen, the window before us open to a faint spring breeze. San Francisco is in one of those rare interludes between winter drear and summer drear. It's almost warm. I suck in air between sips of tea.

"Better?" Tim asks.

"Much."

"How about we go over to the Castro for an early dinner. Ever been?"

I snort a laugh.

"Okay, I kinda figured that, which is why I want to take you there."

It's like he's casually suggested a trip to Mecca. "Fine," I say while the married part of me jabs at such blasphemy. As we dress a whole new set of concerns hits me. Fledgling gay man, I am at a loss out of bed. I feel overdressed in charcoal slacks and white dress shirt but Tim assures me I'm fine. I watch him bypass jeans in favor of khakis and white shirt.

We take a streetcar instead of the underground Muni because Tim likes the old relics collected from all over the world, a colorful assortment trundling up and down Market Street. Soon we're tucked into a small seat on a yellow car that says Cincinnati and I once again enjoy us being a couple. Looking around, I see others like us, old and young, all headed toward Mecca.

The car ends its run at Castro Street. We hop off and there it is. I stand in awe until Tim takes my hand, which makes me issue a nervous chuckle. He holds on, guides me forward.

The Castro Theater marquee announces the new land. Its towering neon spire looms over the block but I'm just as caught by the people. While the setting isn't all that different from Polk—small shops, cafes—it has an energy so distinct that I experience a new kind of rush. I watch people approach—singles, couples holding hands, dogs on leashes, a few children with parents—and I recognize that I am with them and they me, that here in this street, this neighborhood, I can shed the old skin and come into myself.

"So what do you think?" Tim asks.

"It's like Disneyland."

He laughs and squeezes my hand. As we stroll past a hardware shop and bookstore, bank, dry cleaners and all the usual neighborhood shops, I note among them bars, adult video stores, leather specialty shops and I can't help but feel I've been caught over the line when I know full well there is no line here. As I gaze at a window display of leather harnesses Tim mercifully does not ask if I'd like to go inside. He does suggest it when we come upon a noisy bar where I get the idea he may be known.

"Maybe some other time," I manage, too many eyes upon me. Tim guides me on, still holding my hand. I don't think he gets it that the hand-holding is, for me, the equivalent of the bar and leather shop rolled into one. "How about we get that dinner?" I suggest.

We agree on something simple and double back to a diner called the Cove on Castro where we order burgers and fries. I find myself gawking like some tourist but I can't get enough of the male couples. I also note how quiet and calm and consistent they are, eating and talking so easily while inside me the amusement park gates have been thrown open, hordes rushing in.

"What?" Tim asks when I stare too long.

"I don't know. It's just another neighborhood and yet it's so much itself, so distinct, so definite and sure. The idea that I might be allowed in is almost too much to believe."

Tim nods.

"I think maybe I've found a home," I add

He reaches across for my hand. "Good. Good."

Later, as we eat, I tell him I'll make the call to Maureen when we get back to his place. "She deserves the truth," I add, "but for now I just want to take it all in. You included."

THE BIRDS AND THE BEES

Alpha Martial

I'm not usually big on the significance of numbers and the like, but staring absently at the calendar, I just noticed that today is the eleventh of November—the eleventh day of the eleventh month—and it so happens to be exactly eleven years since I first met Jenner.

The way he used his surname as his first name like that reminded me of those damaged public school boys who would attempt to cover up their insecurities by clinging to the custom that had marked them out as privileged in their eyes. Okay, so I don't know many men who've retained the habit into adulthood, but my grammar school sixth form had played host to boys from the third-rate public school down the road; for some reason, they couldn't teach their sixteen to eighteens so they sent them to plague we *lesser* folk whose parents thought that a good education was more important than rituals involving crumpets and whips. Does it show that I resented their presence? But in any case, Jenner was no public school boy; he just didn't like to be called Darren. I tried Daz on him a couple of times, but if it hadn't been for my larger build, I think he'd have decked me. I don't like to feel like a bully, so Jenner it was.

I'm trying to write my monthly column for the *Kent Courier* and finding myself unusually distracted by almost anything. It's because I'm trying to avoid appearing too hard-line on the subject the editor strongly hinted he wanted me to cover this month; it's supposed to be a gentle kind of column. So, today, I pick thoughts of Jenner—or of *then*, at least—for my distraction. If he were here now, he'd roll his eyes at me and grimace before disappearing outside for a smoke. His lack of understanding of my studiousness and favored subjects bordered on aggressive at the beginning of our relationship and only got worse as it trundled on its merry way to the finish.

"How can anyone get passionate about carrots?" he'd wonder in his most ignorant, whining tone. "I mean, even the most interesting possibilities are boring!" (Obviously he'd never reached the very depths of deprivation.) I can still visualize the way he'd shake his head, making the bleached tips of his trendy haircut tremble just ever so slightly. He wasn't vain, but one did get the impression that he never made a gesture or a move without first running it by his own personal image police.

It's hard to believe he came from a background and locality not that dissimilar from my own. In fact, he'd lived pretty much next to open countryside, as I did. For me, its pull has always been inexorable; Jenner was different.

With a great sense of timing, a green woodpecker chooses to fly past my window, a flash of scarlet and lime, cackling as he goes. Finally, the task in hand loses ground again (hell, the deadline's not until tomorrow evening) and I devote myself to reverie...and questions. I've never stopped asking them—always the same ones—and, as the years go by, I have to wonder if this continued inquiry is ever going to yield answers. Is it him I miss? Or is it *there*? The *him* part, well, it was doomed to failure, wasn't it? Didn't stop it from being fun…at times.

As for *there*, that's another matter entirely. *There* is technically only an hour-and-a-quarter's drive away if you put your foot down; I'll go at the drop of a hat for any other purpose. But the idea of being part of the community is now so far away in a psychological sense that I seem to hit a block just trying to focus my attention on the possibility. Am I scared? Perhaps, yes.

My days at the preeminent agricultural college of southeast England were spent in rapt enthusiasm. I guess I was a late developer in other ways. I've spoken about this with other rural gay boys and they all say the same thing, at least to some degree: it's not easy to get experience. But most of them at least seek it; that's why they all go *there*, usually at the first opportunity. A libido just sufficiently indignant to drive me plus my belongings the hour-and-a-quarter and a million light-years necessary insinuated itself much later for me. I was twenty-two before I finally went to London for anything other than a day trip; I accepted a two-year research post at a city-center uni. Sure, I wanted the masters, but I could have made a more appropriate choice of institution.

It wasn't until much later that I learnt that gay societies in the city universities weren't the sorry affairs that they were in provincial ones, which only appeared to attract the politicos—and membership in which could lead to ostracism. Succumbing to the temptation that had drawn me to the city in the first place meant, as far as I was concerned, setting foot in *those places* I'd read about in *Gay Times* and *Attitude*.

And what a picture I must have presented. I've been told that I give the impression of having sprouted from the earth itself—no bad thing for a farmer. But my idea of city clothes meant wearing a new T-shirt and my faithful old leather jacket, polishing my newest walking boots and buying a fresh pair of the cheap-but-practical jeans I always wore. All this topped off by an unruly mane of thick, dark hair. It sticks out from my head almost perpendicularly and I cut it once a year, when I remember; I think I'd forgotten the year before. It's been pointed out that I behave as though I don't really exist in the same dimension as everyone else; that I seem to express surprise when someone acknowledges my presence. I'm not sure how this happened; I don't lack confidence in myself and my abilities, though it's very true that I don't think too much about my physical impact on the world.

So, you see, when I first turned up at the World's End in Camden (chosen because it seemed to resemble a normal pub; places with huge dance floors were too scary) I was completely unself-conscious. It had taken me well over a month since my arrival to summon the courage and I was there to look on—to think about the possibilities whilst acting the invisible voyeur. It was as though I had complete faith in my control over what happened to me and when. I'm aware of that trait, and of its foolishness, now.

I sat with my pint—some cold, foam-headed apology for real ale—and sneaked glances at the other drinkers between paragraphs of *The Guardian*. My first impressions? Well, they weren't like the motley crew I'd met at the gay soc (and who was I to talk?). In fact, after the second pint, they seemed pretty much what I'd expected (and hoped)...and they all seemed to know each other. What's more, with every inquiring glance that came my way, my comfortable sense of invisibility diminished. I felt like the guy who'd ended up there by accident, some educated farmer in the city for a day, propping up the bar with my broadsheet. There were too many curious glances for comfort. Then, four pints in, someone took pity on me.

Tom was a kind-eyed beanpole of a boy who, I suspected, talked the hind leg off every donkey he'd not yakked into stunned silence before; yet I could also tell that he was loved. Whether or not he ever got laid was another matter. From the subsequent accounts of his friends, I suspect not; he just had his head elsewhere. I warmed to that, but I didn't fancy him. He was too...asexual. If he had liked to come to the country, or I'd gone to the city more than I do, maybe we'd be good friends to this day, but I lost touch with him shortly after I last saw Jenner.

To cut a potentially very long story short, it was via Tom that I met Jenner, though it took me a year. In the meantime, I slept my way through almost every mutual friend of theirs—quite a number for a nonchalant sex tourist like myself. That night it was a guy called Duncan; he had the honor of deflowering me. He was a muscular glam boy from a rich family in Hertfordshire—a bit of a precious sort, as I later discovered—and not the greatest companion for a first-timer. Not to say that I was, literally, a first-timer, but I can't really count the odd furtive fumbles in my early teens. There'd been two of them on separate occasions with different boys, but neither of them identified as anything other than straight so I ended up feeling a bit dishonest, if also satisfyingly subversive. I'd known I was gay from the age of about three.

Still, Duncan was probably the first indicator of my real-life taste in men. When I was younger, I always seemed to be attracted to the classically handsome type—the sort of guy you'd see illustrated on the covers of old Mills and Boon books. My mother used to hide a stack under her bed like evidence of a secret perversion. I even read a few, but the way the heroes were written didn't live up to the brooding beauty shown in the pictures. A good lesson—but I put it down to the odd phenomenon that is M&B. Duncan looked like a modern version of those depictions, with shorter, overstyled hair, dark-lashed and bright blue eyes and a mouth which, though sensual, could be said to betray his self-centeredness. He was businesslike in his approach to sex; a couple of years ago, I happened to learn that he'd become the editor of the biggest British gay porn magazine, which made a lot of sense. He insisted on calling me "Jeremy," after the singer of the Levellers, he said (though Jeremy was actually the bassist; clearly Duncan wasn't an aficionado of crusty rock) and asked to take me back to his Finchley flat around five minutes after monopolizing me. Jenner was actually there that night; the memory of his face haunted me until I saw him again, but I didn't get the chance to speak with him. And Duncan was good-looking enough for me....

He made us both a vodka and Red Bull before smoothly relieving me of my clothes between slurps. I sat on his sumptuous bed (the studio flat wasn't much more than a bed-sit, though richly furnished) feeling tipsy and slightly bemused as he—equally smoothly—removed his own jeans and shirt. It seemed I wasn't remotely expected to do anything but service him. We knew the barest facts about one another and exchanged just one short kiss before he quickly worked his way down over my chest to suck me to attention. That didn't take long either. I was kind of shocked but more than ready; I'd been waiting twenty-two years, after all—and never expected such a pretty guy to look at me twice. When he said he wanted me to top him, a wave of panic hit me. I told him it was my first time; he said he knew and it didn't matter. And indeed it didn't; he talked me through the approach, the entrance and how not to shoot my load in five seconds, and Bob actually *was* my uncle. As a how-to guide it was exemplary; as a meaningful experience, it was lacking.

From that night, I came to learn, quite quickly, that I could be seen as the archetypal Real Man—in the sense of being strongly built and having a complexion grace of a lifetime spent mostly outside. For a lot of gay guys—epitomized by Jenner—even if they grew up in the countryside, they shunned that lifestyle. So maybe I represented that country hunk who was ever unattainable—the one who could give them the shag of their lives...but wouldn't. Back in the country, once I'd learnt from my time in the city, I've managed to capitalize upon it no end; I read those fleeting, longing glances and give out the right signals in return.

In the muted autumn daylight that managed to make it through the window the next morning, Duncan looked almost every bit as much of a catch as he had through seven pints. If I had a hangover, we'd worked it off before I knew about it. Duncan went off to work happy; I went back to my flat to clean up and eat breakfast before my afternoon seminar. Life had changed; it was as though someone had put a new lens over my vision, subtly altering the hues of everything I saw. The grim streets—all that horrible concrete, the pollution-stained old buildings—ceased to feel quite so claustrophobic, albeit temporarily; the grays took on a greenish cast which made me feel happier, less alienated. Plus there was the invite to another night out that Duncan had casually thrown at me as we parted. He'd made it clear, without being too unkind, that he wasn't expecting a repeat of our night of passion; apparently he had a policy. It was no problem to me. The last thing on my mind, at that stage, was a relationship.

And so my London social life started. Duncan and Tom were

part of a nebulous gang who'd been hanging around together since the start of their university years. In the meantime, there'd been leavers and joiners—some of them boyfriends and ex-boyfriends of existing gang members, some of them who just happened to tag along. There were a couple of fag-hags, as the harsher amongst the guys called them, though I personally found their company on nights out a welcome diversion from the endless politics of the group. Later, I found out that the two loudest critics of the girls had each slept with one of them...you can never trust a misogynist queer. But on the whole, I liked my gang, as they became; they taught me how to enjoy the city—how to forget my homesickness for precious stretches of time—and how to have sex in every conceivable place and fashion.

And, for the first time, I didn't have to hide that part of myself all the time. I'm lucky in that it's not the most important part of my life, and that I've never felt that my sexuality is evident to strangers. I've never had to pretend to be someone I'm not, on the surface; school wasn't a trial. If I could meet the right partner, we could pretty much live here without anyone knowing the details. In rural England, that's still necessary, but at least it's possible for me. I treated my time in London like a secondary degree course, with modules—apart from the aforementioned—including *General Clubbing*, *Small Talk*, *Looking in the Mirror Before Going Out*, and, yes, even *Dancing* (I never did *too* well on this one, funnily enough). As with the majority of degrees, most of the modules are pretty useless when taken outside of the context in which they were taught. And I was painfully aware of that, then as now; success in finding a partner is made infinitely easier close to the scene....

However, as the months in the city rolled by and I found myself less and less immediately needy, the countdown to the end of my four semesters began in earnest. I went home every few weeks, but the yearning still wasn't satisfied. My masters was largely a business management course, but I'd ensured that the subject for my dissertation was agricultural; in my second year, this meant that I could escape even more regularly to further my research and catch some fresh air. The problem was that every time I escaped, I was less and less willing to return.

How can I express it? Perhaps if I give just a couple of examples of why I'm so comfortable in the country... There is the light at night, for example; in the city, it's either glaring white or putrid orange. There is no break from it—and why? Apart from the fact that stumbling and falling on concrete hurts, there's the ever-present fear of other people—too many of them in too small a space. So you're forced to sacrifice any connection with the stars and the phases of the moon and meanwhile the muggers and rapists can see you more easily. Then there are the birds. City folk are so detached from their sounds and their implications that they even chase the few surviving species from the stations and pavements in case disaster strikes over their new outfit. How could I ever learn to prefer the drone of traffic to the "monotony" of a chaffinch or a blackbird? Every sound in the city assaulted me after a few months. Each to his own; Jenner made me accept that, but I will never understand. However it pans out, my life is about more than just people....

When my father died after a long battle with cancer, my desire to leave London was no longer merely for selfish reasons. My mother was already sixty-five years old; I was their only child, an afterthought in their forties. I'd been involved in the running of the farm since my midteens; it was already virtually mine and my mother was exhausted with the running of it. We had two good employees, but I needed to get back to take over.

It was with all of this going on in my life and my head that I met Darren....

He'd been to Australia for a year, working in a Sydney bar. By the time I met him, he was a sophisticated twenty-four-year-old, confident in his identity and his place in the world—so he'd have you believe. And I guess I liked that in him at the time…just as he seemed to like the contrasts in me—the fact that I was happy in the skin I was born in and didn't have that need for *sophistication*. I wonder if he sees it the way I do after all these years, or whether he'd still tell me, not in so many words, that the aspect of me he most appreciated simultaneously made me a less than fully formed gay man in his eyes. He'd tell me he couldn't touch me for cool and self-assurance but I could read the subtext so easily; I was cool and self-assured because I made no effort for my image. That made me uncivilized.

We met in the World's End, funnily enough. I might have taken it for déjà vu, but when we were introduced, Jenner said he remembered me from that first night too. He took my hand in his and shook it lightly but meaningfully, holding onto the ends of my fingers just a little too long. It would sound arrogant had I not already explained my experience with the rest of the gang, but there was very little doubt in my mind that I would be finally sleeping with this boy that night. And how right that he should be the last of them….

It wasn't that he was spectacularly beautiful or anything. Is it ever like that—I mean, when you're acting on instinct rather than merely beauty-hunting? (I've met a few guys who do that.) He had a rich kind of face—one that suggested we'd have things to talk about after sex. He probably would be technically termed attractive too: his skin was a perfect texture, his lips worthy of Caravaggio; there was an intense, intelligent look about his deep brown eyes. And he was giving me those looks—the ones I was too green to interpret the first time I saw him across that crowded room a whole, long year before.

When I managed to break the spell of our first mutual appraisal, I immediately asked him where he'd been—managing to leave off the *all my life*, which he promptly filled in for me. We both laughed, but we knew that destiny was knocking. When Jenner looked at me like that, I was there. The lightest touch of his fingers on my forearm resounded throughout my body. Yet we didn't rush into anything; it was three intense evenings later that we actually went home together. Even then, we took it slowly. It had to be savored.

There followed almost ten months of passion, tenderness, arguments, understanding, love and incomprehension. I guess you might call it a standard relationship in those respects. Or maybe not. Looking back, I know that from my side of things, the situation back home and that whole yearning sometimes gave me more of a bear's head than I'm normally guilty of. Perhaps I was also grieving for my dad. But Jenner was in a different league. I never knew where his head would be from one day to the next, and we saw one another most evenings even before we moved in together. He'd taken a job in media sales—a not-so-great use of his upper second-class degree, as he knew—and he was always hyped. As far as he was concerned, my work was not only pointless but easy for me. He was right in the latter sense. But thank god I'd always managed to stick to my rule of finishing study by seven o'clock; if I'd tried to work with him around, it would never have happened.

Two hours every night were spent unwinding Jenner from whichever convoluted mental position he'd got himself into that day. After that, there was the occasional added debate about what we were doing together. After that, there would be something to eat, something to drink, possibly an outing, then sex. Weekends, thankfully, weren't quite so stressful; without them,

I think we'd have split up after a few weeks. As it was, those weekends became the vertebrae of our relationship, connected by vulnerable cartilage and nerves. It was odd, and fascinating, the way the rest of the gang treated us after we got together, like a crowd parting to watch an impromptu spectacle. On three occasions, I was propositioned by guys who'd previously snubbed me; Jenner had the same experience, though, in his case, the numbers were higher. My possessiveness didn't make things any calmer. I tried to curb it, but, in my defence, I was in love, and for the first time. My comparative maturity made no difference. Perhaps there was also an element of self-preservation on a more serious level; we'd been tested together twice, and dispensed with protection. Despite our long conversations about the rightness or otherwise of our partnership—maybe because of them—we both felt we were in it for the duration.

During the eight months together before the end of my course, Jenner came home to Kent with me only two times, each for only two nights. My mother disliked him on sight and told me so, but made nice with him because, as she put it, it (he) was my mistake to make. I think she was rather glad I was gay; if she was critical of men, it was nothing compared with her ferocity toward women. Add to that the fact that I was her only child and it became comparable with the fabled paternal protectiveness over daughters. I suppose that was my first real eye-opener with Jenner—seeing him around someone I knew so well and could read so easily. Having said that, I'd have thought her behavior was hard to miss. He just didn't clue on; he really thought her good hostess act was genuine. Was he actually so dumb that he couldn't see falseness that blatant? Or was it more a case of his having built up such a sturdy self-image—like a firewall around himself—that anything unpleasant or threatening just bounced away unnoticed unless it were spelt out explicitly and allowed entry? On the one hand, something a work colleague or client would say to him could upset him so profoundly, yet he'd miss all the signs when I was unhappy with something he'd done. Jenner forced me to be more verbally combative than anyone I've ever known. What happened with my mum made me realize why.

Other than that, for those first visits home, we had a good time and I had no reason to acknowledge the gaping chasm between us. I believe that everyone needs to feel the open air sweeping across landscapes not peppered with tall buildings and human ruination—even if they're not aware of it. Jenner certainly benefited; the overt tension seemed to float away those first two times. Between tasks on the farm, I took him out walking, showed him all the secret places I'd known as a kid and pointed out various plants, insects and birds. The fact that he even seemed interested in the things I was telling him—like remembering to rub his arm with a dock leaf when he got stung the second time by a nettle—gave me hope for our future.

On one occasion, during the second visit, we were lying naked in a hollow under the oldest oak tree on our land. I'd had sex, as I mentioned, in all kinds of places in London—on trains, in City side streets abandoned by their worker occupants at night, in the tiniest of parks; even, once, in the classic toilet setting—but I hadn't so far had the opportunity to fulfill one of my ambitions since childhood: to have someone join me in exposing myself to my most familiar piece of sky. It was early summer and surprisingly warm. At that instant in time, we seemed blessed.

Jenner loved to be in charge most of the time, though, for me, he made exceptions. I guess that was another of the attractions for me; he wasn't easy. Very often, I let him take the lead because I enjoyed it. But that time, in my domain, on my ancestral lands, he laid himself out like a platter full of goodies. It had happened before but, touched by the breeze and the filtered sunshine as we were that day, it was as though a precedent were being set. I thought I was bringing my lover home....

For once not fussing about his surroundings, he looked more dashing to me than ever—if completely incongruous—on his carpet of crisp dead leaves. I lay on my side next to him and traced his dark, arched eyebrows with my ring finger, staring into his eyes all the while. He was trying to close them, but couldn't. It had been his idea to get naked yet, somehow, he seemed cowed by our environment, as though it stirred memories of boyhood trysts and humiliation. He never spoke about them, but I knew they'd happened. What made me think I could overcome their legacy, I'm not sure. Blind optimism? Yes, that's it. As for my more literal vision, it was so perfect that afternoon that the images will probably stay with me forever.

He finally looked at me, simultaneously stroking his fingers along my side, over my waist and hips, then down. He flicked me one of his careless smiles, though I knew he felt anything but that, and pulled me into his space. He never tasted of smoke when I kissed him, oddly—always fresh. I took him over, pushing my tongue inside him like the definitive act of possession. He responded with arms around my back, finally succumbing to the present over the past. Does that sound too Mills and Boon? Never mind; it's how it happened (though perhaps my old secret reading habits will always creep into my reporting style).

Sometimes I felt that kissing Jenner was the only way we ever managed to profoundly bond—which doesn't say much for our mutual communication skills; it was the only way to ensure we neither spoke to nor looked at each other. But no, it was more than that; it really was special—like positive meditation. I've never found it with anyone else, hard as I've tried, and I know it was as much me as it was him; the chemistry, rather.

That particular kiss was the best I remember; it went on and on, deepening with each tightening of our hold on one another, with every investigative touch. Maybe I was more relaxed than Jenner, knowing that we were far from any footpaths crossing the land and that Mother was likely to stay in the village with friends until the evening. He knew these things but didn't trust them as I could. Initially, this danger seemed to intensify his excitement, but he was no exhibitionist; after several minutes, as the hypnosis of the kiss began to fade, his excitement turned to urgency. I think I could have carried on for days....

Afterward, I felt his reluctance to lie there like that with me for much longer. He lit a cigarette and glanced around us, that dizzy expression echoing my own return to the everyday plane. I brushed his come across his belly, feeling dampness amongst the hairs on my chest where the rest of it had landed. He looked at me suddenly, drawing hard on his fag.

"You know, I could never live here. All this green makes me feel conspicuous." Echoing my earlier observation, he dropped his little bombshell with barely a flinch. Obviously it had occurred to him that our time together would be limited if that didn't happen...but maybe he just expected my love for him to make me change my soul and live in the city for good.

"We could always compromise—do fifty-fifty." He nodded slightly, uncertainly. How could I manage the farm part-time? I'd only been able to get my head around it because I felt it was important to finish my qualification and things had been ticking along okay; once I took the reins, that would be it. What's more, I didn't want it any other way.

Picking our way through fresh nettles on the little path back to the big path, I tripped over a hidden bramble and almost fell flat on my face. Jenner stopped behind me and took my elbow.

A green woodpecker piped up at that point, cackling its tiny red head off. "They always seem to do that at opportune moments..."

"What do?"

I explained.

"Green woodpecker..." he mused out loud. "Are you all right?"

"Yeah, fine." To Jenner, falling over a bramble was simply something that had never happened to him; or if it had, he'd stashed it away along with the rest of his unwanted memories. He couldn't help it by that stage; it was an alien landscape to him. It was during those last few months that I began to realize another truth: Jenner had forced himself to fall in love with the city and the effort had been so gargantuan that any other love had to take second place. At that point, in my condition, I hadn't the wisdom or clarity of mind to put it all together. There was still hope. I felt that my real love for my favorite place must be strong enough to counter his fabricated one.

And I called *him* arrogant...?

We tried, we really did. We made it through eight months and Jenner was getting sick enough of his horrible job to think about jacking it in. I dreamt of a time when he might be a relaxed person in the evenings—when our social life wouldn't have to be a drunken distraction from his days. And his unemployment coincided nicely with the end of my studies. I'd had long discussions with Mother about his moving into the farmhouse. She'd go along with it, putting in little remarks about her remaining "queen," et cetera. "Jenner's not a queen!" I protested. To which she somberly replied, "He's the type to turn into one, given half the chance." But behind her comparatively compliant act, I knew there was complete faith in the fact that it wouldn't work out anyway—that Jenner really wasn't going to last more than a few weeks here, at best. She didn't want to say as much. I had to make my own mistakes, of course.

We even tried the fifty-fifty thing, after a fashion. I still had the two guys on the farm whom I could trust implicitly—well, one of them, at least, and the other did what he was told efficiently. But it seemed more like five days in the city, two on the farm, and every night away became more and more painful for me. I was torn. Darren couldn't keep on much longer without money; both his social life and his fashion sense demanded it and, in turn, his job search demanded that he not stray too far from town. I held out hope that, once he'd found something, he wouldn't mind commuting every day. Crazy. Finally, I persuaded him to take a break from it for a week with me.

I tried to prevent him from his attempt to pack his entire life into two suitcases. He was adamant. "There has to be a decent place to go out down there, surely? If there is, I'll find it…." As if I wouldn't know. I tried to picture him, all dressed up, in one of the provincial straight clubs I'd been to on odd, unfortunate occasions.

"We can come back here for that any time we want to," I offered, hopefully.

"…Between sheep dips. Okay."

"Well, you can be preening yourself while I'm dipping the sheep. The timing should work out about right, and I won't look any different from what I normally do. Might smell a bit, but whatever." He laughed. We always laughed easily. I took that for a good sign, right until the end.

August. In England, not even August is reliably gorgeous, but that year it was. I felt full of optimism as we drove down, Red Hot Chili Peppers blaring, in Jenner's soon-to-be relinquished

Audi A4. As with many aspects of our lives, in that short time together, we'd already shared so much; I was listening to obscure house and he'd developed a tentative taste for all things rock and indie. I think he was secretly relieved just to be getting away from the pressures he was putting on himself at home. I had more hopeful visions of a U-turn on his part and maybe he *was* thinking the same. In any case, it was a joyful ride....

The first night of our little holiday, once he'd got over his slight pique about my spending two hours checking things over on the farm, was probably the most passionate we'd had—aside from those when there'd been an all-out argument beforehand, in which case the sex was usually more like violence. With the window open to the cool, night air and the moonlight breaking through the sparse clouds, the good old romance novels came into my mind again. And Jenner could pass for one of those heroes in that light. All my fantasies seemed fulfilled...and under the right roof.

But I was fooling myself. And Mother, as usual, was right—except for the fact that it didn't take weeks; it took days. As he squeezed his two cases into the boot of the car and turned to me to say good-bye, a familiar cackle drowned out the ambient birdsong. I smiled at him, hoping to elicit some kind of positive last word...but he'd forgotten. Perhaps he never took it in for more than a few minutes—long enough to comment at the time. My face fell. He took my hand briefly and said, "See you when you get back."

Get back? I *was* back.

He left, skidding out of the drive on the summer dust, careless of which of our unsuspecting cats or dogs might run under his wheels. I turned to Mother, who was staring anywhere but at me.

I saw him only twice after that. I'd moved into his flat, so things were less complicated than they could have been if he'd moved into mine. The sum total of my possessions fitted into roughly the same volume of luggage as he'd brought on that last trip. It didn't take long; two hours to remove almost all traces of a relationship we'd kidded ourselves was for a lifetime. But neither of us was in doubt anymore. His words had been decisive. In my local pub, some drunken mechanic I'd known since I was five started aggressively questioning my choice of friend: "He's a fucking shirtlifter—look at him." When Jenner turned and walked out, I assumed it was in disgust. But when, after shaking my head at the culprit, I'd followed him into the car park, I recognized the expression all too well: fear. And how could I blame him? As he pointed out repeatedly over the next couple of hours, the threat wasn't directed at me—oh no: "You're the perfect closet case." And effectively, he was right....

It wasn't the biggest row of our time together—not at all. It was as though we both knew, all of a sudden, like a spotlight on the truth this ignorant man had inadvertently turned on. It was bigger than both of us. The solace I find in the country is the equal and the opposite to that which he found in the city. Maybe he's not lonely like me; part of me hopes not—part of me hopes he found a job that was good for his self-respect and a partner who really fit. But part of me is fiendishly jealous of his possibilities as I imagine them. *There* is where guys like me should go; it's one of those undeniable truths in life. All the one-night stands I've had over the years have been city boys who happen to pass through or those in potential; they never stick around.

As the melancholy sound of a tawny owl warming up for the evening greets the darkness outside, I contemplate, for about the thousandth time, going up to London for just one night—just to see if a miracle happens. I've never done it. And one answer I might be starting to accept, after all this time, is that I've never gone because I really did love him; I can't imagine anyone to compare. If a broken heart is the best the city can offer me to make up for its coldness, I'm better off alone....

GOD HATES TECHNO

Zeke Mangold

There he was, pushing a cart of ice down a carpeted hallway in search of Room 177. Bored, he paused in front of a mirror near the guest elevator to reenact a scene from *Taxi Driver*: "You lookin' at me?" Dell plopped into a chair, lit a Marlboro, and listened to the Killers' "Somebody Told Me" via the ceiling's tinny speakers. He thought yanking a fire alarm might cut short his shift, but couldn't recall where the cameras were. Probably they'd already captured him ashing in a potted plant.

"The iceman hateth," he said to no one.

Summer had burned its way to an end, and Dell's pool lifeguard position at Baja Palace Hotel & Gambling Oasis evaporated. He transferred to food and beverage, working five nights a week as a barback in a motorcycle-themed nightclub called Throttle that infringed heavily upon Harley-Davidson Café. What did he care? He wasn't toiling in a Boulder Highway casino for its originality. He worked as a barback because he wanted to make money and maybe get his dick sucked by one of the chiseled flair bartenders who specialized in slinging liquor bottles à la Tom Cruise in *Cocktail.*

Truth be told, Dell wasn't that experienced. Sure, for a few weeks he tussled with Gus, a security guard who went on to accept a better, higher-paying position at a lavish casino on the Las Vegas Strip. Gus aside, Dell hadn't enjoyed much action since coming out the previous year, just before high school graduation. Spending his teenage years on the edge of the valley in the conservative suburbia of Summerlin had only intensified the dirty downtown sex hunger driving his fantasies. Now, he longed to drill a hole in the wall of the gay bookstore inside Commercial Center and take on all cummers.

For the moment, however, he was busy transporting ice to a private party as a favor to the F&B director. Seemingly out of nowhere, a new Nevada health law required all personnel—in other words, Mexicans—to get their hepatitis shots before dealing with ice. Dell had been inoculated at the university, so he was asked to deliver the cold stuff to the VIP suite, where, more than likely, a bunch of sales-industry hags were rinsing and powdering their dried-up labia for a night in front of the slot machines.

So he was surprised to hear reverberating bass emanating from Room 177. He had to pound the door viciously before his arrival registered over the chaos.

The music stopped. A slender, good-looking blond wearing sunglasses opened the door. He said nothing, looking confused.

"You order ice?" said Dell.

"Ah. Yes." The man stepped out of the doorway so Dell could wheel in the cart.

A turntable and speakers were set up in the room. Empty pizza boxes and drained beer bottles littered the surfaces of things.

"Partying solo tonight, huh?"

The man shook his head. "Nah, my friends are already at the

club. I'm spinning later tonight." He picked at something stuck to his tight black T-shirt, while Dell admired the taut muscles of the man's arms.

"At Throttle? Hey, I work there."

"Bartender?"

"Barback," Dell said with a shrug. "Where do you want the ice?"

"Leave it there," said the DJ, making his way to the turntables. "I need to figure out something first."

Not wanting to return to the club and slice lemons, Dell asked, "What do you spin?"

The DJ had already donned his padded earphones, but heard the question. "Mash-ups," he said, arms crossed, staring intently at his mixing board. Stymied, he turned to Dell, looking him up and down. "Got this a cappella thing—the Carpenters' 'On Top of the World'? But I can't make it work with anything."

Dell thought. "Well, you know, the Geto Boys had this nasty track back in the day called 'The World Is a Ghetto'..."

The DJ snapped his fingers. "That's good." He began typing on his MacBook Pro, no doubt downloading the song from the Internet. He smiled at Dell, extended his hand, and said, "Name's Bugsy."

"Oh, DJ Bugsy!" said Dell, reaching forward to shake. "I was reading about you in the weekly paper the other day."

"Yeah, um, Throttle isn't the snazziest club in Vegas, as you probably know. But at least they pay me to spin what I like. Do you have to work right now? Grab a seat, man."

Dell did indeed have to work, but instead reclined on the couch and flipped through an issue of *DJMag* while Bugsy remixed the wildly divergent songs, fusing them into something unique and slamming. When it was ready, he removed his headphones and blasted the unholy coupling through giant speakers, Karen Carpenter's voice sounding unusually sexy as it mounted the wild rhythms of Scarface and Bushwick Bill.

"Evil," said Dell.

Bugsy nodded with complete satisfaction. "Lethal."

Bugsy saved "On Top of the Ghetto" for the end of his set at Throttle. Dell was carting a tub of glasses to the dishwasher when he heard Karen's voice ("Such a feeling's coming over me") followed by the explosive Geto Boys beat. He looked over at Bugsy, who reciprocated with some kind of gangsta sign that meant nothing to Dell.

Whatever. Bugsy was still super-hot. Forget the Throttle bartenders.

Wrapping up his set at five AM, Bugsy invited Dell to a downtown diner. They ate cheeseburgers and discussed hip-hop until nearly noon, though the younger barback didn't listen to much of the genre other than Public Enemy, N.W.A. and, of course, the Geto Boys. Somehow they got on the subject of the gay nightlife scene in Vegas, and he remembered the article he'd read in the paper: Bugsy spun at the major gay clubs in town. Clearly, Dell had a shot at fucking the shit out of this adorable DJ.

"The city is where the action is," Bugsy said at one point.

"Since my mom and I moved here three years ago," said Dell, "we've lived exclusively in the 'burbs. What's it like downtown?"

"It's amazing. You'll see."

Dell and his friend London spent Sunday afternoon at Lock N' Load, where you could shoot a real machine gun in a concrete, air-conditioned range. London was developing an obsession with firearms, and Dell thought it suited her. They had lifeguarded together at Baja last summer, but now she worked as a stripper, making three thousand a night at Garden of Eden

Gentlemen's Club. She loved the money but hated the clientele. A dude had spooked her in the parking lot as she was getting into her car, which led to buying a Glock. Which led to her joining a gun range. Which led to Dell being here, donning safety glasses and ear protectors and pointing a Thompson M1A1 at a paper target of Osama.

Even though he'd bought two hundred rounds of ammo, he quickly emptied his gun. An instructor retrieved his target, and Dell noticed only a few bullets had hit their mark.

"Fuck," he said, pulling out his protectors. "I couldn't hit the side of a barn."

"It's because you're cockeyed," cracked London, reloading her Uzi. She had her hair pulled back, safety glasses angled on her nose, and her rack looked stunning in a Radiohead T-shirt. He loved the way her breasts bounced in tandem with her gun's short, violent bursts. It was almost enough to make him want to kiss her.

"I've got more than cock in my eyes."

"Yeah," she said. "Balls."

"You're jealous, right? Just because I'm having dinner tonight with a musician."

London slammed the cartridge like an A-Team member and smirked. "Please. A DJ is not a musician. DJs steal other people's music. They're glorified plagiarists."

"What's wrong with plagiarism? It's how we made it through high school."

"Excuse me," said London. "I'm Asian. I don't need to cheat. And another thing."

With that, she raised her Uzi one-handed and blasted a paper target of Saddam with five clean, efficient burps. Because he wasn't wearing protectors, Dell flinched and may have actually pissed his boxers a little.

London pouted her lips and blew on the gun barrel. "God hates techno. You're not in high school anymore, Dell. Be careful out there."

"Aw, you really do care about me." He couldn't hear her reply for the ringing in his ears, so he added, "Maybe Bugsy and I will get an apartment downtown."

London snorted and proceeded to reload.

They dined on Chicago-style Italian at a little hole in the wall in the downtown arts district. Having never been on a formal date before, Dell didn't intend to order anything with garlic. But since Bugsy was slurping *escargot* with gusto, Dell caved in and scarfed down some garlic bread with his spaghetti and meatballs. It tasted great.

Bugsy poured Dell a glass of red wine, and the barback downed it in a single gulp.

"Hey, slow down, gorgeous," said Bugsy. He'd finally removed his sunglasses, revealing dreamy blues eyes.

Dell felt good in the presence of this sophisticated soul, a DJ who had performed in clubs across the globe, from Ibiza to Iceland, and who now enjoyed residencies at clubs up and down the Strip as well as downtown. At the same time, Dell's heart went out to an artist who could find his truest expression in a second-rate nightclub on Boulder Highway.

"You're right," said Dell. "Sorry."

"No worries. It's Sunday. We've got all night."

Dell's dick quivered.

He soon found himself giving Bugsy sloppy head in the DJ's Land Rover behind a warehouse on Commerce Street. Dell performed a Lewinsky by popping an Altoid before going down, giving Bugsy's engorged cock a new sensation.

"That's nice," said the DJ.

To give his jaw a rest, Dell gently nibbled on Bugsy's nuts.

"Deep-throat me," cooed Bugsy.

He pushed his cock into Dell's mouth, hitting the back of his throat. Dell opened wide as if to yawn, and took Bugsy as far down as he could. He let the DJ's cock rest there, holding down his thighs to keep him from thrusting deeper. And then Dell did something he hadn't thought he was capable of—contracting the muscles in his throat and massaging the head of Bugsy's penis.

"Oh god," Bugsy whimpered.

They moved the encounter to a mattress inside the warehouse. Bugsy threw a few beach towels over it and propped a flashlight against a crate for a sexy, if somewhat sinister, atmosphere. He pushed Dell onto his back and gave him an incredible rimming. Dell lay with his legs spread. Bugsy kneeled down and pushed Dell's ankles up, carefully guiding himself in. Gradually, the DJ accelerated his thrusts, pumping Dell's tight bum.

"I love watching my dick go in and out of your ass," said Bugsy.

Dell bit his lip. "Go as deep as you can." With his legs up, Dell came when Bugsy began sucking his toes. The DJ's deep penetration must have stimulated Dell's prostate, because he exploded, his wad splattering his own chest. Bugsy licked the cum off Dell's nipples.

"My turn," said Bugsy.

"In my mouth," said Dell.

Bugsy pulled out and stood up, fiercely clenching his dick to keep from spurting. Dell got to his knees, greedily vacuuming the knob just in time for the first blast of liquid love.

"Mmm." Dell purred as Bugsy's cum flooded his mouth. He swallowed dutifully, but Bugsy was firing off so fast, so thick, he couldn't keep up with the ejaculation. Cum flowed down from his chin where it had spilled from his mouth, and more of the stuff oozed down the sides of Bugsy's penis, toward the hand Dell had wrapped around the shaft to hold the DJ steady while he creamed.

Dell's fist was sticky with goo, and slowly he worked that fist toward his mouth, scooping cum as his hand moved, his tongue roving about, searching for more.

"Good boy," said Bugsy.

Afterward, they showered at Bugsy's apartment and went back out into the desert night, dancing at Tarantula, a new nightclub on Fremont Street. There, Dell met an endless parade of local promoters, managers, and other DJs. They were all friendly, offering Dell drinks at every opportunity. Dell passed, wanting to keep his wits about him.

"Your friends are nice," he said to Bugsy.

"They're the best. But they have a mischievous side, too. You'll see that on Friday."

The music got the best of him, and Dell danced with most of Bugsy's friends until three AM. Dell loved house, but Bugsy wasn't impressed.

"I've heard this set a million times," he observed on the drive back. "He had people dancing, sure. But he's not transporting them anywhere."

"Where do you like to transport people?" Dell asked.

Bugsy thought about it. "Someplace different. Someplace they've been curious about but never had the courage to explore. I want to be their guide."

"Speaking of," said Dell. "I want to get my own apartment downtown."

Bugsy looked at Dell before fixing his gaze back on the road. "You should move in with me for a few weeks while you're searching."

Dell felt his heart skip a beat. "That sounds good. Thanks."

The next day, Dell insisted London join him for a shopping excursion at the outdoor mall near Main Street. They visited every store, including Baby Gap, and ordered ice-cold Frappuccinos to cool off in the heat.

"This can work," Dell insisted. "Everything I need is within walking distance."

From behind her Ray-Bans, London still managed to shoot him a look of profound disgust.

"All right, biking distance then."

"Dell, you're a product of the suburbs. You won't last five minutes in this part of town."

"Are you kidding? Look, here's a Banana Republic."

"If you want to move out of your mom's house, fine. But maybe you should choose an area that isn't overrun by homeless people?"

"No one is homeless here. And you're being insensitive. Besides, London, you're the one who works downtown."

"Why do you think I bought a gun?"

"Well, I'll get a gun, too. I was considering a pearl-handled revolver."

"You would."

"When I find a place, will you help me move?"

"Why don't you get your boyfriend's boyfriends to do it?"

"Now that's an idea."

Friday arrived, and Bugsy invited Dell to the Zone, an established downtown gay bar that boasted a drag queen revue starring Stacey Shockwave. One of Bugsy's friends was in charge of the show's lights and music, and Bugsy admitted that he and his buddies often threw jerk-off parties involving Stacey.

"He's a total slut," said Bugsy over dinner at Andrea's, a French bistro just a stone's throw from City Hall. "And he looks great, whether dressed as a man or a woman."

"Where do you guys jerk off?" asked Dell, feeling the rush of blood to his groin.

"Usually in Stacey's dressing room. You're hard, aren't you?"

Dell said nothing, using a fork to pick at his salad. Bugsy reached under the table and put his hand on the barback's lap.

"Up for a party?"

Dell shrugged. "If you are."

That night, Bugsy and five of his friends—mostly bartenders and bouncers who also lived downtown—made their way to the Zone. Stacey Shockwave ended up putting on a hell of a show impersonating Madonna and Gwen Stefani, while her fellow performers nailed Celine Dion, Bette Midler and Britney Spears. Dell despised drag shows, but he had to admit this one was pretty first-rate. In between numbers, he chatted with Bugsy's friends and admired the guys walking around with colored shots at five bucks a pop.

After the show, Bugsy pulled Dell out of a conversation he was having with another club-goer.

"Time to party," he said, a wicked expression on his face.

Dell followed Bugsy out a side door and into the parking lot. It was dark behind the club, and Dell saw Stacey squatting in the shadows before a group of men, sucking off a guy he'd been talking to earlier in the club. Stacey had wiped off his makeup and removed his wig, and Dell noticed that, with his sharp cheekbones, he was deadly attractive, even while wearing a miniskirt and fishnet stockings. And with his face stuffed with cock.

The guy standing over Stacey moaned loudly, obviously unloading. Stacey sucked him dry. Then he stood up and kissed the man hard, snowballing the man's own cum into his eager mouth. Instantly, another man, a stocky dude with big biceps, stepped forward.

"Cum in my mouth," Stacey said, back on his haunches. He opened wide and said, "Ah."

The eager man unzipped the fly of his jeans and pulled out a nine-inch dong. The others unzipped and began stroking themselves.

Stacey sucked cock with a ferocity Dell had seen only in the nastiest porn movies. One by one, Bugsy and his friends stepped up and let Stacey suck them to a powerful climax. But now the guys were pulling out and jerking off right onto Stacey's tongue.

"Don't swallow until the last guy's finished," said Bugsy.

Watching Stacey catch the jizz of at least six guys in his mouth almost forced Dell to squirt early. But he slowed his stroking enough so he could watch the black guy in front of him shoot yet another thick load into Stacey's hungry maw.

When it was his turn to blow a wad, he stepped up and stared right into the queen's spooge-slicked mouth. Stacey did his best to smile, given the quantity of cum soaking his tonsils, and pressed a finger against Dell's prostate, enhancing his pleasure. Dell could smell the other guys' semen. He brought himself to a righteous orgasm, lowering the head of his cock into Stacey's mouth and spurting huge white ropes, which were promptly gargled.

"Swallow it," Dell said. "Swallow it all."

Stacey did just that, wincing at the enormity of the collected load. "Oh, fuck," he said. "That was good and salty."

"I'm not done yet," announced Bugsy. "Bend over."

As the drained guys stumbled back into the bar for more alcohol, Stacey leaned forward, one hand on the Dumpster and the other raising his skirt. Bugsy spit in his hand for lubrication before plunging deep inside. Stacey had been rock hard for some time and now, with his skirt raised, his own man meat was on full display. Bugsy started hammering Stacey's ass the same way he did Dell's.

Dell couldn't help himself. He knelt down in front of Stacey and began furiously sucking. Stacey immediately erupted, his sweet jizz making Dell want a double load himself. He reached between Stacey's legs to touch Bugsy's sac, which was still slapping relentlessly against Stacey's ass. Dell felt Bugsy's balls tighten.

"Pull out," said Dell. "Let me taste Stacey's ass mixed with your cum."

Bugsy was already spurting as he switched holes, shooting a small but succulent wad directly onto Dell's lips.

"God, I want more," said Dell, wiping the jizz from his face. His heart was pounding, and he could feel blood rushing in his ears, at his temples. He remained on his knees, in shock at his own performance.

"Next time," said Bugsy. He and Stacey smiled, the two of them patting Dell on the head like he was a puppy.

An hour later, Dell phoned London as he filled up his Honda Civic.

"You won't believe what happened to me," he told her.

"You bought a pearl-handled revolver," quipped London.

"Tonight a DJ changed my life."

"So now downtown is the place for you?"

"It definitely has its advantages," he said.

LOCAL FAME

Ted Cornwell

It's beginning to trouble me that so many of my dreams are set in a city where I spent a few precious years of my youth, a city in which I haven't lived for twenty years. In some dreams, I live in houses that are absurdly large, with views of downtown and a veranda for sipping iced coffee during the humid summer. In others, I reside in a firetrap of loose floorboards, leaky plumbing and menacing strangers who apparently are my roommates. Sometimes, friends from my life in New York intermingle with people I knew back then. Last week I had such a dream—of sitting around with contemporaries, and suddenly X, my first boyfriend, walks in the door. He seems to know everyone in the room. Later in the dream, X and I are sitting alone in a winterized porch with floor to ceiling windows. It is snowing outside. X shows me his camera. It looks like a big old Polaroid, but he turns it over and begins to scroll through digital images on the back of the machine. He's showing me photos he took that morning. The photos are of naked young men, sketchy and tough looking, who lean against rocks or tree trunks with their arms folded and their sex willfully exposed. They frown back at the camera. The pictures have been taken along the Mississippi River bluffs between downtown and the university, where dense forestry mixes with industrial ruins to form a particularly seedy and alluring landscape. Even though it is snowing outside in the dream, it is summertime in the photos, and the naked men are sweaty and honey-tanned. Suddenly, I look up and one of the young men from the photos, one of the most ornery looking, is standing outside the window, in his winter clothes. He and X stare at each other intently. I fear he might try to break into the house, but instead he pulls down his pants and masturbates, spurting onto the window in front of us. I wonder if I should be jealous of his connection to X, who watches indifferently.

There are many other dreams of course. But lately, they often occur in some version of Minneapolis.

There were four of us—me and three girls—giddy in that van that decamped from Decorah, Iowa for the glittering Aphrodite lights of Minneapolis in June of 1987. In the months leading up to our graduation from Luther College, none of us had any idea about what to do or where to go when school ended, until Jane came up with the brilliant idea of Minneapolis. Her friend Nancy, a few years older but like us a graduate of Luther, lived in a duplex near Lake Harriet. Her two roommates had moved out, and she would let us stay there, at least for a while, for just a hundred and fifty dollars per month for each of the two available bedrooms. Stacy and I planned to share one room; Jane and Melinda would be in the other.

It all went swimmingly for about two and a half weeks. Nancy was cosmopolitan enough to know where and when hip events were happening and collegial enough to invite us along.

We went to parties where other recent college graduates and migrants to Minneapolis gathered to swap job leads and troll for dates. Kegs of beer were hoisted into garbage cans full of ice. At one party we met a novelist, much older than most of the crowd and mildly lecherous toward some of the women, who claimed to be a Vietnam veteran. At another event, we saw a performance artist take off all his clothes and declaim the poetry of John Berryman while beating on a rather plangent, homemade drum. Stacy was rebuked for giggling.

On the ride home, I was consulted on the question of whether or not the performer, whom we knew only by his stage name "X," had been aroused during his performance, or whether it was natural for a penis to "stick out like that," as Stacy put it. My verdict was that X had a "semi" when he first took off his clothes, which softened as the performance got underway. Jane concurred, saying his penis did seem smaller by the end of his show. She then listed an unlikely assortment of penises she'd seen, including Paul Newman's in a movie about Alcatraz, and her brother's, peeked at through a bathroom door keyhole. There had been a sculptor at the party who was widely esteemed in the Twin Cities art scene. He was said to be forty years old but looked younger. Jane and he made quite a scene in the back alley behind the miniscule theater where the performance and after-party had occurred. This, as it happened, turned out to be the downfall of our domestic arrangement.

The next day, Jane and Nancy had quite a row. It turned out that Nancy—whether or not this was known to Jane remains a mystery to me—had a substantial history with the sculptor, which included passionate lovemaking, bitter breakups, periods of platonic cohabitation, and eventual estrangement. She accused Jane of seducing him out of spite, or allowing him to seduce her out of spite. Melinda came into our room, where

Stacy and I huddled on one of the beds trying to decide whether it was best to leave and give them space or to stay put with the door closed and pretend not to exist. We chose the latter option. Phrases such as "dog whore" and "anorexic shit-face" were bandied about. The culmination of the fight came from Nancy: "Get the fuck out of my house! I want you and your friends out of here." Doors were slammed.

We sat in shocked silence for some time, and Melinda started to weep. Eventually, she was the one who broke the silence. "What are we going to do?"

Neither Stacy nor I had an answer to that.

Jane moved in with the sculptor the next day. Stacy found a studio apartment in Saint Paul. Nancy, having calmed down a bit, told us to take our time. With Jane's help, I found a group house on Ridgewood Avenue that had an opening. The day I left I saw Melinda and Nancy sitting at the dining room table, both weeping quietly. I thought I heard Melinda say, "I can't believe he did that to you."

"It's not the worst that's happened to me since I came here," seemed to be Nancy's reply. I said my good-byes hastily and dragged my two duffle bags out to the waiting taxicab.

Weeks later, Jane received a postcard from Melinda, who had moved back to Decorah. In the note, Melinda said she'd seen city life, had witnessed its callous cruelty and casual squalor, and never wanted to live within sight of a skyline again. She gave her regards to everyone and said she was planning to become a teacher.

With my khaki slacks and penny loafers, I was a bit of an ill fit in that rickety Victorian mansion on Ridgewood Avenue, which was precariously perched on a litter-strewn slope above Highway 94, with downtown Minneapolis marooned on the other side of the freeway. But they said the house had been standing since 1894, so I decided not to worry about its foundation. There were eight bedrooms, and someone else was temporarily taking quarters in what had once been a formal dining room. The residents fell into three camps: homosexual men, vegan women, and a small posse of bisexual nudists. There was an old icebox, which the vegans actually filled with ice and used to refrigerate their soy milk and bean curd. I did not realize that the performer X was among the residents until I moved in, and I quickly observed that he more than anyone was able to maneuver freely between the house's cliques. I learned that his real name was Christian McLeod, which sounded nearly as exotic as his stage moniker. When I was in the entry vestibule alone, I would thumb through his mail, fingering the letters addressed to him. Some people in the house called him Christian, some called him X. I asked which he preferred.

"I prefer whichever you like best," he said.

The only bona fide couple in the house, Tory and Dean, were landscape architects—though they said their jobs usually involved scooping up dog poop from the yards of dowagers who lived in mansions near Lake of the Isles. They took a paternal liking to me, and I began to quiz them about X. "Be careful around his kind," was all Dean had to say. "Oh, for crying out loud, he's young," Tory interjected, pointing at me. "Don't be so prudish. Let him have some fun."

"Just don't let him break your heart," Dean warned.

I had made the mistake of telling my housemates about my job at Kinko's, which I described as a management training position. They didn't know whether this made me an exploitive yuppie or just showed that I was easily duped into working overtime without pay. In any case, most days my shift started in the early evening, which gave me time to lounge around the house or pursue my interest in photography during the day. I took pictures of sagging old houses around Powderhorn Park. I documented the squalor of bridge underpasses, freeway exit ramps, and anything else I considered spooky or existential, having read Sartre in a senior year philosophy class.

At the house, I increasingly looked forward to any encounter at all that I might have with X, who often lounged in the sunporch down the hall from my room or wandered about in an oversize bathrobe that he didn't bother to tie shut. He had been reading Kierkegaard and Kathy Acker lately, I noted. X was tall and sandy colored, too thin for some tastes. Few thought him beautiful, but then again few averted their eyes. In my case, initial intrigue was morphing into complete infatuation. I resolved to win his attention, and did it in a manner I thought he would respect. I decided to become a nudist.

Which is to say, wrapped in a towel on the way to the bathroom, when I had assured myself that there was nobody else nearby, I deliberately allowed the towel to slip off my waist as I passed the sunporch, feigning embarrassment. If X noticed, he didn't give any sign of it, and continued reading.

So I had to up the ante. I sat by my window the next morning, counting off as residents and their guests left the house. Some few, who were home during the day, had to be tolerated as a risk factor, but I was careful to consider their schedules and listen for the creaking of floorboards. X took his perch on the old divan in the sunporch, its upholstery lacquered with age. My heart began to pound. I took off my clothes and stood inside my room, so exhilarated by the thought of walking naked past X that I immediately became aroused, and the cautious Iowan inside of me screamed not to take such a dare. Think of the things people will say about you, my inner voice roared. You'll be the talk of the house, for crying out loud.

On the other hand, nothing ventured, nothing gained.

I pulled the door open and stood there, excited beyond all telling, knowing that X was just steps away. To fortify my courage, I recited, as best I could remember, Henry V's Saint Crispin's Day exhortation to his troops. I then stepped into the hall and turned toward the sunporch and the bathroom beyond. As I came into the opening in front of the porch I felt the hot sunlight washing over my pale flesh.

"Whoa," X exclaimed. "The shy boy is bold today."

I giggled and hurried on my way, closing the bathroom door quietly behind me. I took a lukewarm shower. As my erection faded, I wondered whom X would tell about my little exhibition. When I was done, of course, I had no towel. It was a contingency I had not planned for. I had to go back naked as well. I shook the water from my hair—it was long in those days—and made the return trip.

This time I looked in at X. He seemed to be waiting for me, sitting up with his bathrobe open. He beckoned me toward him.

"So what brings this *joie de vivre* on? Not that I'm complaining," he said.

I said something along the lines of "I dunno." I looked at him and he looked at me. The sight of his hazel eyes scanning my body excited me, and I became aroused again, letting him watch me rise. We both laughed a bit.

"It's about time you loosened up," he said, standing and slipping the terry cloth robe off his shoulders. He cloaked me in the robe to dry me off. Then he took it back and spread it down on the divan, asking me to sit down with him. I sat right next to X. I told him he was sweet to let me dry off on his robe. We held hands and then we held each other's cocks and kissed very passionately. In the intensity of the moment, I forgot that anyone else from the house could walk right by us. X leaned me back and laid himself down on top of me, face-to-face, and I don't think we stopped kissing at all during this repositioning.

Afterward, we cleaned up after ourselves, applying a damp cloth dipped in Woolite to spots on the old divan, but I was proud that a small stain remained, hardly a lonely one on that old piece of furniture. But I knew exactly which one represented the abandonment of my virginity.

For six months, we lived in a kind of coital bliss. I had practically abandoned my room in favor of his. He taught me positions and the practical aspects of seduction and foreplay. X was not ashamed to discuss these things, and the opportunity to instruct seemed to excite rather than dampen his enthusiasm. Everything seemed to be going fine, until I started prodding him to think about the future. Perhaps we should get a place of our own, I suggested.

X, who was on the verge of turning thirty, did not like talking about the future, making plans or commitments.

"I really want to be with you, only with you," I told him.

"Let's just take things one day at a time," he replied quickly, patting me on the head. He was sometimes quick to silence me with a long kiss, and he wasn't afraid to slip a hand down my boxer shorts at the same time. I learned to recognize these signs that I should stop talking.

But I was old-fashioned. Iowa mores were drilled into me, and I found myself trying to inject them into my bohemian lover. When X had an affair with Chaka, a vegan and a Wicca practitioner whom I had presumed to be a lesbian, it struck me to the core. I demanded that we move to our own apartment. He suggested that we cool things down, and admonished me for wanting commitments that I might later regret. What could I say? I thanked him for the brochures he gave me about a photography class at the MacPhail Institute. He did, after all, take more interest in my photography than anyone else in the house, or outside of it, for that matter.

During this "cooling down" phase, X spent less time in my area of the house, and seemed to have abandoned the sunroom altogether. He even started fastening his robe. Often, I found his door closed when I passed his room.

I was heartbroken, but stoic. I read *Anna Karenina*, rather prominently, hoping he'd notice and recognize my distress. But he was very busy applying for grant money and rehearsing a new performance piece. He spent more time away from the house than before. Word got around that he was seeing someone, a graphic designer famous for producing one of the early album covers for a local rock band that itself had gone on to national fame.

By the start of my second winter in the old icebox house, relations between us had thawed into a begrudging friendship. X even stopped by my room occasionally to look at photographs or drop off a flier about an upcoming show, and he was less fastidious about tying up his bathrobe than he had been in the months immediately following our split. Once, we even revisited the past, you might say, when he'd stopped by to return a book and found me in my bath towel. But we were both apologetic about it afterward and heartily agreed that it didn't mean anything.

That was at the start of the winter when I became famous, and when everyone else got fed up with the cold and decided to leave town.

The weather turned bad in November, and stayed bad through April. It began with the biggest blizzard I've ever seen, one that closed schools for two days. As soon as the snow stopped falling, I put on my snow boots and went out with my camera to document the carnage. I photographed the lumpy outlines of cars in white burial mounds; snow like inchworms lining telephone wires, like lichen covering bare tree branches; snow reflected in the glass of office buildings; snowdrifts barricading the doors of houses; sloping piles of snow that seemed to drag mansard roofs down from houses. Jane, who also worked at Kinko's now, helped me make postcards with the photos. They sold like hotcakes. The Café Weird on Lake Street invited me to enlarge some of the pictures for a show. These larger works all sold as well. All of a sudden I was the "snow guy." The weekly tabloid *City Pages* even printed a small feature about my triumph, publishing a couple of images from my blizzard portfolio. At parties and gallery openings and even in the artsy sort of pubs, I was suddenly somebody who was known. It helped that I was young enough not to hear the slight tone of condescension when more avant-garde artists told me that my photos were "cute." I was just glad to finally be someone about whom something could be said.

But even as my star was rising, the exodus of those I held dear had begun. Jane herself was the first to go. A psychic told her boyfriend, the sculptor, what he'd known all along: now is the time. After twenty years of dreaming about achieving a national reputation, he needed to reach for the stars. The two of them packed up an old station wagon, scraped the frost from their windows, and headed east to New York. Stacy didn't actually leave the Twin Cities; she just disappeared with her fiancé into one of the outer suburbs stitched to the fringe of the metropolitan area. X was the shocker. As he hadn't worked in any conventional sense for years, I wondered where he contemplated getting together enough money to move to California. But he and the graphic designer did just that, with an eye toward getting involved in independent films. Around that time X had also turned his attention to standup comedy, reasoning—perhaps correctly—that performing nude after the age of thirty wouldn't draw as large a crowd as it had in his twenties. (In truth, he still had a lean and attractive body, but audiences were dropping off because everyone who wanted to see him already had). They hitchhiked to L.A. in March.

"Not to worry," Dean of the landscaping duo told me. "Most of them will be back by June. It happens every winter. It gets cold. People feel pent up with cabin fever. Everyone says they're leaving for one place or another, but most of them don't go. And of the ones who do leave, half are back within six months, complaining about the crime or the smog or the high cost of everything where they went."

He suggested I should just wait it out. But wait for what? I was already famous in Minneapolis, but I didn't know what my next act was.

With X gone, I began frantically searching for love. I looked in coffee shops, at gallery openings, at the Gay 90s or the Saloon and even at the 19 Bar, but I found none. Instead, I was reduced to walking briskly past crowds near the dance floor, puffed up with attitude, just to see if I could turn heads. (Jane had taught me this trick.) I felt abandoned and shell shocked, especially when spring came and none of the migratory exiles returned as Dean had promised.

In the heat of July, I returned to photography almost obsessively, after abandoning it for a few months to revel in my fame. I took summertime photos of the exact locations covered in some of my famous blizzard photos, and paired the photos together. But this tripe did not startle anyone. I began photographing people—with their permission—hoping to break new ground. When I first saw Adrian, feeding pelicans from a pedestrian bridge over a small pond in Loring Park, I knew I wanted to shoot him right away. Of course, I also knew that I wanted much more than that. Adrian was black, and he had bleached the tips of his dreadlocks orange. He allowed me to photograph him sitting on a rail of the bridge, beside a pelican that was not afraid of people, with the IDS Tower in the background. His smile was guarded and flattering at the same time, like that of someone taking a dare or telling a secret. He was the most beautiful man I'd ever seen.

Adrian showed me a flier for his band, Same Time, Different Place, with a mimeographed picture of himself with two white girls. They were opening for Babes in Toyland at the 400 Club, so I knew they must have some kind of reputation. "I'm the boy in the girl band, or at least the girly boy in the girl band," he explained. I'd never heard of his band, but my knowledge of the local music scene did not extend far beyond Prince, Husker Du and the Replacements.

Adrian was much shier than X. We talked for a long while in the park before I ventured to invite him back to Ridgewood Avenue, and we talked for an even longer time seated on my futon before I dared to touch his hair. I don't think we started undressing each other until we'd driven down every conceivable lane of conversation at least twice. We kissed and giggled and got used to each other's skin for a long while. I was amazed at how easily one could stumble upon sex in the city, how it might just be waiting for you in a park on the edge of downtown. I didn't think to call it sex, though. I thought, *I've stumbled upon love*. I thought this as I was licking his nipples—he had the most sensitive nipples of any man I've ever met. He actually gasped when I kissed them.

The next morning, he came into the kitchen with me, grinning a bit sheepishly as we navigated around assorted housemates. I showed him the icebox that the vegans used, and he said he'd seen iceboxes in old houses before, but never one that was actually used.

Little did I know that the wheel of fortune was already spinning. Two days later, before Adrian and I had the chance to reconnoiter for a second date, I received two urgent phone messages from Jane in New York. I called back figuring she wanted a favor, perhaps for me to send something. But it was much more serious than all that.

"His roommate is moving out at the end of the month, and he's so sweet. I can't believe it, Fred. You'll be living right across the hall from me."

"But Jane, I can't just leave right now. Things are starting to work out for me here. I've got irons in the fire. I'm planning to reprint some of the blizzard photos for Christmas cards."

"Take the irons out of the fire and get your butt to New York. You can't really make it as a big-time photographer in Minneapolis. I know there are some exceptions, and I know it sounds snobby, but to really become well known as an artist you have to be known in New York."

"I need to think about it for a while."

"Think about it? Fred, do you have any idea how hard it is to find an apartment or a sane roommate in New York? Both just landed in your lap. Move here, if it doesn't work out you can always move back."

"But I don't even know this guy you want me to move in with. Shouldn't I meet him or something?"

"There isn't time. But guess what? He's from Iowa. It's perfect. His dad taught at Iowa State. He's really into urban environmentalism. You'll get along great."

"Let me think about it for a few days. I just need to process this."

"You can't take that much time. He'll get someone else. I'm going to tell him you want it. I'll front the deposit for you. You can pay me back when you get here. I'm giving him the deposit tomorrow afternoon. So if you change your mind, call me before then. But don't change your mind. New York needs you."

After we hung up, it occurred to me that perhaps Minneapolis needed me more.

What sealed the deal, however, was the assurance that my roommate-to-be was from Iowa. Though I had no interest in going back home, I retained a provincial faith in the goodness of people from Iowa.

When I called Adrian, I told him what I believed to be true: that I'd be back in six months. I was just going to get my feet wet in New York, take a photography workshop if I could, explore the city's cultural landscape. But I was committed to being part of the Minneapolis scene. After all, I already had a reputation and some clients. I don't recall exactly what Adrian said, but he seemed stunned that it was all happening so fast.

After last week's odd dream, with X and the scary exhibitionist, I started a massive Google manhunt for everyone I remembered from my salad days, when I was somebody in Minneapolis. I'm single again, and I have the leisure to look back ruefully. I've been back in touch with X, via email, ever since city-loathing Melinda, of all people, updated me on his whereabouts in a Christmas card. Melinda had become friends with our brief first hostess, Nancy—don't ask me how or why—and Nancy had told Melinda that X had given up his old stage name and was now doing performance poetry in L.A. using his middle and surnames: Alex McLeod. I like that there is still an *X* in his name. But I had not kept in touch with the other people from the old icebox house and beyond.

Tory and Dean have an Internet billboard advertising their gardening business. In the photo, they look much older but every bit as merry as I remember them. Chaka is running for city council as a Green Party candidate. Stacy is teaching sociology as an adjunct at a community college.

As for Adrian, I've tried everything. The problem is, truth be told, I never learned the last name of the love of my life. So I Google search "Adrian" and "Minneapolis" or "Adrian" and "music" or "Same Time, Different Place," and I wade through a sea of Internet flotsam and find nothing relevant except a few postings about the band performing at First Avenue in the early 1990s. There's no roster of band members, not even a photo.

I was at a party in Jackson Heights last weekend, and I found myself thinking, Adrian could be here. Not at the party, I mean, but here in New York. He seemed like the type who might have made his way here eventually. I'm at an age when parties easily irritate me. There is always at least one person there who is much younger than me and whose work is being shown in well-known galleries. They tend to be loud talkers. I can cope with my lack of fame, but the loss of my youth has left me bitter. I went up to the roof of the building, where some people from the party were smoking. I sat by myself looking back at the Manhattan skyline. I buoyed my spirits by scanning the city and thinking yes, Adrian could be out there someplace. He could be walking around tonight in this vast sea of lights and concrete that I have learned to call home.

ABOUT THE AUTHORS

RACHEL KRAMER BUSSEL's books include *Caught Looking*, *Hide and Seek*, *Crossdressing*, and the nonfiction collection *Best Sex Writing 2008*. Her writing has been published in more than one hundred anthologies; she's senior editor at *Penthouse Variations*, hosts In The Flesh Erotic Reading Series and wrote the "Lusty Lady" column for *The Village Voice*. Find out more at www.rachelkramerbussel.com.

DALE CHASE has been happily writing male erotica for nearly a decade, with more than one hundred stories published in various magazines and anthologies. Her collection of Victorian gentlemen's erotica, *The Company He Keeps*, is coming in 2008. Chase lives near San Francisco and is working on a collection of ghostly male erotica.

TED CORNWELL is a poet, fiction writer and journalist who grew up in Minnesota and has lived in New York City for the past decade. His fiction has appeared in *Dorm Porn* and *Best Gay Love Stories 2006: New York City*, and his poetry has appeared in the queer journal *modern words*.

JAMESON CURRIER is the author of a novel, *Where the Rainbow Ends*, and two collections of short stories, most recently *Desire, Lust, Passion, Sex*.

ERASTES lives in the UK and was a punk in London in 1977, but will only admit to being too young to remember. His gay short stories have been published in collections as varied as *Ultimate Gay Erotica*, *Treasure Trail* and *Superqueeroes*. His first novel, *Standish*, was nominated for a Lambda Literary Award. www.erastes.com.

LEE HOUCK was born in Chattanooga, Tennessee and now lives in Queens, New York. He has written original pieces for theater seen in Vermont, Tennessee and New York; an essay appearing in *From Boys to Men*; and poetry featured in the Magnetic Poetry Calendar. Additionally, he has created art installations for the Musée de Monoian, and has worked with Jennifer Miller's Circus Amok for ten seasons. He is at work on a novel. For more, go to www.leehouck.com.

ZEKE MANGOLD has been a Las Vegas blackjack dealer for twenty-two years. He took up writing late in life, having wasted his youth in dark desert taverns all over the Southwest; his first published erotic fiction appeared in *Hot Cops*, and he is working on an erotic novel set in Las Vegas, tentatively titled *Casino Queen.*

JEFF MANN's work has appeared in many literary journals and anthologies. He has published two collections of poetry, *Bones Washed with Wine* and *On the Tongue*; a book of personal essays, *Edge*; a collection of poetry and memoir, *Loving Mountains, Loving Men*; and a volume of short fiction, *A History of Barbed Wire*. He teaches creative writing at Virginia Tech in Blacksburg, Virginia.

ALPHA MARTIAL is a Brit now living on a smallholding in rural France with his long-term partner. When not preoccupied with vegetables and chickens or busy as an artist's agent, writing is his favorite pastime. His short stories have appeared in several anthologies, including *Best Gay Erotica 2005*; his first novel, *Sappho and Tulle* (coauthored with Romy Were), is an exploration of sexuality and fantasy. A selection of his fiction appears on http://telltale.free.fr.

DOUGLAS A. MARTIN is the author of two novels (*Branwell*, *Outline of My Lover*), a volume of short stories (*They Change the Subject*), and two collections of poetry. He is also a coauthor of *the haiku year*.

SAM J. MILLER is a writer and a community organizer. His work has appeared in numerous zines, anthologies, and print and online journals. He lives in the Bronx with his partner of six years.

KEMBLE SCOTT is the author of the best-selling novel *SoMa*, based on twisted true tales from San Francisco. He is an alumnus of the Columbia University Graduate School of Journalism, the editor of *SoMa Literary Review*, and has three Emmy Awards for his work in television news. His website, www.kemblescott.com, features videos shot at the real-life places that inspired the novel, including the locations depicted in this excerpt. Kemble frequently speaks to book groups and organizations. You can reach him directly at: kemblescott@gmail.com.

SIMON SHEPPARD is the editor of *Homosex: Sixty Years of Gay Erotica,* and the author of *In Deep: Erotic Stories; Kinkorama: Dispatches From the Front Lines of Perversion; Sex Parties 101* and the award-winning *Hotter Than Hell and Other Stories*. His work has appeared in about two hundred and fifty anthologies, including many editions of *The Best American Erotica* and many, many volumes of *Best Gay Erotica.* He writes the syndicated column "Sex Talk" and hangs out at www.simonsheppard.com.

ALANA NOEL VOTH is single mom who lives in Oregon with her ten-year-old son, one dog, two cats, and several freshwater fish. Her fiction has appeared in *Best Gay Erotica 2007* and *2004*, *Best American Erotica 2005*, *The Big Stupid Review* and *Literary Mama*.

ABOUT THE EDITOR

RICHARD LABONTÉ writes book reviews, edits books, translates technical writing into real English, and reads a lot. Sometimes he's sitting on the porch of a two-hundred-acre farm in Calabogie, Ontario, co-owned with several college friends for more than thirty years. Sometimes he's sitting on the deck of a home on Bowen Island, a short ferry ride from Vancouver, British Columbia, owned by one of those college friends. Often his husband Asa is sitting with him. Email: tattyhill@gmail.com.